This Passover or the Next I Will Never Be in Jerusalem

This Passover or the Next I will Never be in Jerusalem.

by Hilton Obenzinger

batiks by Lisa Kokin

Momo's Press 1980

Sections of this volume have previously appeared in *Omen from the Flight of Birds: The First 101 Day of Jimmy Carter* (Momo's Press), and "Jewish Socialist Critique."

Cover by Jon Goodchild
Typesetting by Eileen Ostrow

Library of Congress Cataloging in Publication Data:

Obenzinger, Hilton.
    This Passover or the next, I will never be in Jerusalem.

    1. Jews—Literary collections. I. Title.
PS3565.B36T5   818'.5409   80-20986
ISBN 0-917672-13-5
ISBN 0-917672-127 (pbk.)

Funding for this volume was made partially possible by grants from the National Endowment for the Arts, a Federal Agency, and the California Arts Council.

Momo's Press
P.O. Box 14061
San Francisco, California 94114

Contents

Why Is This Jew Different from All Other Jews?

This Passover or the Next
I will Never be in Jerusalem

The clan is all together, eating Passover matzoh, joking.
At the head, the old Patriarch makes his blessing; he collars me,
& he imparts wisdom:
"Is it so bad to be a Jew?
In Israel even the street sweeper is a Jew, not that anyone
should be a street sweeper, but
nobody yells 'Dirty Jew!'
After 2,000 years we have something finally. Isn't it about time?
We are not taking any Arab land from anybody.
This is the land that belonged to our forefathers,
& we came only to take up our inheritance.
Can anyone say we are *stealing* what is already *ours?*
Why don't you go to Israel, learn something about your people?
Can it be nothing but good?"

I fidget & nod politely at his references to Abraham & other
    long-lost relatives.

"So you move so far away from your parents in New York,
you move to California to live with the Indians.
You decide to be so noble to be a schoolteacher with the Indians.
Nu, I wish them well, but what is this with the Indians,
aren't they so different & so wild?"
                                        "Actually,
Indians are not what you see on TV . . . "

"Nu, but are they your own people? Your own flesh & blood?
Do you hate New York so much you have to live with Indians?
What is this Indians? You can work in your father's store,
make a good life. He is getting old, and you need gelt in life,
right?
Is it so bad selling rags?
Can't you be writer all you want, love Indians all you want,
& make money too?
What's this, Indians and California?
If not Israel, shouldn't you think New York maybe to live?"

The young couple across the table from me, recently married
(& living just a few blocks away as does all the family
peppered throughout the Brooklyn neighborhood
so as better to visit one another on Shabbas when one can only
walk & by injunction is forbidden to drive),
these young marrieds smile good-naturedly & ask,

"Don't you feel strange living so far away from your family?"

Why is this Jew different from all other Jews?
I sip my wine. The white table cloth is a vast Jordan.
This Passover or the next I will never be in Jerusalem.
The Jordan flows between me and the land I never remember anyone
    promising me.
No sound can be heard except the occasional wail of some
    wild animal.
I will never step across the shore. *Am I the anti-Moses?*

I jump up from my plate, startled.

"Uh, no, I don't feel strange at all. . . ."

Treblinka. California. Me.

Alone, I watch the fat green Klamath slide down the banks.
I throw the book about Treblinka concentration camp uprising down.
It's well known: *Jews flowed into ovens & died.*
I sob, & my head gushes through rocks & that isolated beach.
My heart flings Treblinka down.
I'd like to hide with salmon and seal, in the trunks of acorn trees.
It's well known: *The Klamath is Indian land, Yurok land.*
Here I am, a Jew from Brooklyn, wailing over
my own dead at a wall of water in California.
The Klamath remembers its own blood.
Without this river, how could there be Yuroks?
What the hell is a Jew doing here, anyway, by what bond?

Suddenly from out of the brush
a deer steps gingerly on the pebbles.
Hid among the rocks, he peeps out to see what's going on.
He watches, alert, but strangely not suspicious.
I stop crying. The deer steps forward, approaching me,
slowly walks, pauses, spies me, pauses,
& walks again.
He nears the river, bends to drink;
his lapping explodes the silent river.
I move towards him, reach out, palm forward to stroke him.
Those soft antler nubs, still furry, please him the most.
I tug & stroke those nubs,
& he wags his head around till he's had enough.
My heart eases.
My companion paces back into the woods.

When the first whites
poked out from the brush
for the first time,
they saw this same beach,
felt it:
"I cannot describe my feeling as we came upon this stream.
We rounded a bluff . . . a sheet of silver . . . flowing swiftly . . .
thick woods grew down from the highlands to the water's edge . . .

an Indian gliding along in his canoe.
This was Sunday and there seemed to be a Sabbath stillness;
no sound could be heard except the occasional wail of some
    wild animal.

It did seem like intruding on forbidden ground."

Yet their hearts constricted, they didn't pace back
into thick woods but lingered, looking for gold, then timber, fish.
They built roads, & I came on them,
a Jew from Brooklyn, here, scanning the Klamath,
the odd white schoolteacher on the reservation, asking.
My companion, the tame deer, has no problem welcoming me.
But I stumble over the obstacles, the ghosts:
Treblinka. California. Me.
Yet it's no use hiding in the trunks of acorn trees,
I might as well pick myself up. . . .

10 years pass.

The Klamath still runs intact,

                        not yet filched to LA,
though I relocate to SF
where there is never Sabbath stillness
& my father, visiting, asks in distress:

"Why are you so much with the Indians and the Arabs, living here
with a woman and her 3 kids, I don't care Jewish or what
3 kids not your own but your responsibility, isn't that so
even so not your own people, a Filipino woman,
and you working in a printing plant with nothing to show for it
except honking your horn at people on picket lines
& waving at strangers
maybe on strike—
why? I don't understand, why?"

                        which is a good question:
                        How *do* you understand?

My father fled Poland despite his father's admonitions
against America's impiety.
So anxious, he unwittingly booked passage to sail
on Yom Kippur day itself.
His mother exclaimed, "So? He's a goy already!"
& the old Patriarch replied, "*Should America need one more?*

> *Better he be buried in the sand*
> *than to be a heathen*
> *in a heathen land . . .*"
>
> Heedless, he set sail.

Now, my father is strung out, like
deer jerky on a drying rack,
suspended between his own father & his son.

So, what the hell is a Jew doing here, doing this?
I'm tempted to say: Why not? It's history!
Do I have to have an answer, isn't fact enough?
But I can't. How *do* I understand?
Sometimes it takes a good 2,000 years
before you get a decent answer.
But I need to know, to have it explicit
as a salmon's eyeball
or a river.

Nevertheless, I watch TV with the future,
5-year-old Kalayaan—

> *)an Indian sheds a tear*
> *for the beer cans crunched*
> *in the stream*
> *weeping for America*
> *to pick up its own junk.(*

She says, pointing to the screen, "That's *your* people!"
I correct her, "Not exactly, Kala."
"Yes you ARE—you're a white Indian!"
"Uh uh," her older brother interjects
in reference to my stories about the Treblinka uprising,
and he explains in explicit words of the Projects,

"Naaaa . . . he's a *concentration camp Jewish head niggah!*"

I look at them, laughing—how they stretch
across chasms of TV on a couch.
Filipinos born in California, I hope they remain intact
despite all our yet inconclusive migrations.
So here I am, plucked over walls of water like them,
a Jew
bound by my responsibility
with others, I don't care Jewish or what, my own people;
despite my father's admonitions, no less
a Jew
baffled by history,
wailing at my own dead, watching, alert,
but strangely not suspicious,
as I wave at strangers on picket lines.

Home on the Range

"Home home on the range!" Hank howls out. His press is whirling at top speed, sheets of paper flinging out the delivery, 20,000 pages of statistics for Pacific Gas & Electric.

"OOOOOWWWWAH!" Hank yells over the din. The pressroom is a monster of noise. When things went right, Hank would always half-sing and half-howl "Home home on the range!" So he stands back, pulls his shoulders back, grins wide despite missing front teeth, brushes his balding grey crew cut, and points to me, "Come on now, lad, let's hear some *real* music—home home on the range, where the deer and the antelope play, WHERE SELDOM IS HEARD A DIS-COURAGING WORD AND THE SKIES ARE NOT CLOUDY ALL DAY." We both howl over the machines and crack up laughing.

"Oh yes yes indeedy that is *real* music, not some of this modern crap," and he strums like a rock-and-roll guitarist, *"Hey hey ho ho Shit on a Hoe Handle Shit on a Hoe Handle*—no class."

20 years in the Navy operating presses on aircraft carriers; now, 55, his hands cracked and raw from the chemicals, he's working at this sweatshop to keep his alimony and his alcohol up to date. And to survive it all, to enjoy it all, he insists on howling like a maniac—all the while scheming to bring the union in. We get along fine.

"But I suppose ilk of his ilk enjoys such trash," and he points at the anti-union college kid working over summer vacation so he can go back to Humboldt State to study biology. "But," Hank continues, "what do you expect from the students at DUMBOLDT State?"

My press gets all jammed up with paper, and I have to yank out the torn sheets and clean off the impression cylinder. My hands are covered with solvent. I've got a cut from handling Polychrome plates, and the solvent stings like hell. Finally I get the machine rolling again. Surprisingly, the conversation held at the top of our lungs has turned to Indian fishing rights on the Klamath.

The biology student from Humboldt State, which is located near the Klamath, is complaining about the way the Indians are destroying the salmon run by their fishing. *"Whoa, wait one minute there!"* I stop him. In bits and pieces I try to explain things. The lumber companies clearcut and silt up the river with debris, clogging up the spawning grounds. The trawler factories off the coast gobble up multitudes of salmon miles before they even reach the river's mouth. The government has plans to dam up the river so as to divert the water down to LA or thereabouts for desert tract-home development. The government doesn't encourage measures to increase the salmon run, withholds funds from Indian hatcheries projects, refuses to regulate the factory-ships, and makes only a show of needling Simpson Lumber. Yet the Indians are singled out because they stand in the way of stealing the river. The government wants to push them out by killing off their buffalo, as in days of yore—in this case, it's salmon—destroying their whole semi-subsistence economy by—

"*Aaaahhh, Indians!*" Hank shouts, "The *dumbest* people that ever walked the earth!"

"Whaddya talking about, Hank?"

"What the hell has a Injun ever done? Gave away all their goddamn land and sit pretty on the government dole? They never had it so good, till we come by. What the hell a Injun ever do? Take the Chinese." He points to the janitor, an ex-merchant from Laos who doesn't understand a word but smiles and nods. "*Noodles! A whole fucking civilization!* That's something to talk about! Invented gunpowder. And sharp too. Jews, they done business with every nation in the world, but not with the Chinese. How come? *Chinese too shrewd!* But Indians—*shit!*"

"Knock it off, Hank!" I try to laugh him off. Undaunted, he keeps on. Either he means this shit or he's just trying to get my goat. Probably it's both.

I squint my eyes at Hank, the impression cylinder of my machine whirling him into a vision of that frenzied line of settlers at the end of the nineteenth century. It's the Arkansas border. Anxiously, they await the opening of "Indian Territory"—Oklahoma—to the land-hungry. I can see Hank there, his foot pawing eagerly moments before the starting gun. He hasn't done anything particularly brutal; others came before. He hungers only to better himself with the grace of a small plot he can call his own.

Boom! The gun explodes, discharges these thousands scrambling into the dust to make their claims. I remember watching it on TV, some afternoon movie after school, a heartwarming Western of honest folks trying to outsmart the bad guys. My eyes bulged. Do you actually mean they lined up and took off, racing to grab parcels and townships? How ludicrous, this starting-line—is this really the way things happen?

I eyeball him. Maybe that was Hank as the camera scanned up and down that line of settlers waiting for the Oklahoma gun. The music was momentous and thrilling as our eyes moved across an endless starting line filled with horsemen and covered wagons. Is that Hank, as the camera pauses, tipping off his dusty hat, brushing his hand over his balding pate, and howling "OOOOOOOOWWWWWWWWAAAA-AAAAAHHHHHHHHHHHH!" over the din? In an instant the camera moves on, leaving Hank to his own anonymous story—the Depression, overalls and no shoes, Navy, too much beer, printing on aircraft carriers, Manila prostitutes. What would he think of Tecumseh, Crazy Horse, or Leonard Peltier if I explained the—?

"Richard Nixon!" one of the pressmen yells out.
"Alright—Richard Nixon! *Pope Richard Nixon!*" Hank hollers.
The pope had just died. The pressroom decided to make our own nominations for the new one. Some names were up on the ballot already—Anthony Quinn and Dean Martin. But others were added to the list—Liberace, George Wallace, Menachem Begin, John Wayne, Miss Piggy, and Dom Mintoff, the Prime Minister of Malta, in deference to the press operator from Malta.
"Pope Nixon!" I shout back. "Haw! Haw!" Sometimes the pressure, the whirling of the machines, the breakdowns punch your nerves to the state of overchewed bubble gum. All of a sudden I get very self-conscious and stop laughing. *A Jew nominating Dean Martin for pope? Shit, I'll get burned at the stake!*

"*Savages,*" the Iroquois exclaimed. "Savages! That's all I ever heard in school. That's what they had in the textbooks, we were all savages."
We were standing around the campfire on the Klamath. The Yuroks and the Hoopas were having important meetings to decide what their next step should be in their fight to fish. The other Indians and the few whites waited around the camp for the results. We joshed around, told stories, trying to get the damp fog sizzled out of our boots. I almost jumped in the fire my toes were so cold.
We had somehow gotten onto the topic of stereotypes. I mentioned I was Jewish and explained some how I felt about it and how I supported Palestine.
"Jews, you're smart, real smart. Don't eat pork. Arabs and Jews fighting seems messed up, like cousins fighting. But, you know, I haven't seen too many rich Jews. (Lemme see, how thick's your wallet —eh?)"
"Shit, they call *us* savages," he went on. "Do you know that we had

a deep healing and hygiene science for thousands of years? When they came, the English, they had a law, a law says no one allowed to take a bath more than *once* a year. Those smelly assholes took one bath a year, they thought it was unhealthy or something, and we have sweats and herbs and all that. And they call *us* savages!

"They never call Jews savages, though, just cheap. Shit, it's just that we knew *psychology.*"

Someone kicked another log into the fire. We could hear the dampness hiss off the bark.

"What do you mean, psychology?" I asked, perplexed.

"Well, they like to say that the Six Nations were exceptionally cruel, like torture and all, against their people. Just not true at all. It's psychology we were really good at. The French, they sent their Jesuits into the land to preach. So this one missionary comes to the people. He talks about his God. The people, they listen, because they respect when someone talks about his god. So he talks more and more, and the people they get together, and they put two and two together. All this missionary talks about is this guy who gets nailed up to a cross and martyrs who died for *us*. They talked it over, and the people *understood* what this man wanted. He talked so much about the cross that they took him and nailed him up to a cross. He wanted to be a martyr, and he got his wish. They nailed him up and, do you know, the people were amazed. HE EJACULATED 17 TIMES, so they knew they were right in what they did!"

Everybody hoots and hollers at the story.

"But you know," he continues over the laughter, "we only learned that trick from you guys. YOU NAILED HIM UP FIRST!"

Ach, stereotypes. How the world revolves around certain stock characters. Hank is wailing "Home home on the range" as I hum a song my friend, Ruthie Gorton, sang to me, the catchy tune her great-uncle, Uncle Harry, sang in vaudeville, 1907, "Yonkel, the Cowboy Jew." You come to America and you learn to be American, right? And what's more American than cowboys? So . . .

> A Jew named Yonkel Finkelstein
> Went out West one day;
> Just to shoot wild Indians
> That's what the neighbors say.

Didn't care a snap for home,
Left his wife and little child,
Met a pretty cowboy girl,
Then his Yiddish brain went wild.

To his friends he sent a note,
And this is what he wrote:

Western life is fine and dandy
I have got no kick;
When I think of the pawnshop business
Oy, it makes me sick.

Every time I see some Indians
I just kill a few,
So I've changed my name from Finkelstein
To Yonkel, the Cowboy Jew.

Now Yonkel made love to the girl
That he met out West;
But she told her beau on him,
And then he did the rest.

With a shooter in his hand
Cowboy made poor Yonkel dance,
Then he yelled, "You tenderfoot,
Run while you have got the chance,"

Yonkel then commenced to pray
And he swore he'd never say:

Western life is fine and dandy
I have got no kick;
When I think of the pawnshop business
Oy, it makes me sick.

Every time I see some Indians
I just kill a few,
So I've changed my name from Finkelstein
To Yonkel, the Cowboy Jew.

Great, just great. I feel like throwing up. *"Every time I see some Indians . . ."* But the moral is, what is a Jew doing being a Cowboy? Ridiculous! Killing Indians is for Wild Goy Bill, not for you. Back to your pawnshop! Back to your sewing machine, schmuck!

Ruthie showed me the sheet-music cover with its two Yonkels. On one side, Yonkel, with beard and suit with diamond stickpin, wringing his hands in front of the pawnshop balls. On the other, Yonkel, with beard, in cowboy suit, looking bewildered and irretrievably lost. How they must have laughed at themselves in Jewish music halls on the Lower East Side!

"It's us, the greenhorns, who are ridiculous, we who are not American." The stereotype becomes real as it turns inward. "You want to be a cowboy, a pioneer? Go to Palestine, kill all the Indians you want over there! *Here* we are slaves, come to thrive in the cities built on the bones of Indians!"

Ruthie and I knock our heads together and moan. Well, that's one strand alongside the sweatshop and socialist songs.

Ruthie tells me the story of a song she wrote. "I was picketing the Israeli consulate in LA with some Palestinians and Iranians. The JDL counter-picketed across the street. Suddenly they tore the placards off their 2-by-4s and crossed the street yelling 'Rag-heads! Camel-jockeys!' We raced down the street, the Zionists at our heels. Later that night I thought I was getting a fever, coming down with a cold, but I realized I was coming down with a song. . . . "

She sings it for me, "Free Palestine Now," her eyes closed, a capella. "To fight against injustice is to be a Jew . . . so free Palestine now . . . free Palestine now."

Who would have thought that, in the twentieth century, we'd become experts on settler-colonialism! Victims of genocide is enough! I recall another friend, Ann, born of Polish Jews in South Africa. She emigrated to Israel a Zionist and then, grown disillusioned, moved to America, an anti-Zionist. It's dizzying . . . Yonkel, the Cowboy Jew, the Bwana Jew, the Sabra Jew. We've been the oppressed so long, but have we ever been the colonized?

"HOME HOME ON THE RANGE HOME ON THE RANGE ," Hank yowls at his press. The college kid from Humboldt State looks at me with slight disdain. What do I know of exalted science and ecology, or, for that matter, what do mere Indians know of such pristine knowledge? He doesn't believe a word I say about the Klamath. I don't have the proper credentials.

My patience runs out. "Ya don't believe me, huh, Bozo?" I shoot back. "You want the river ripped off? Who do you think killed the buffalo? Sitting Bull?"

The kid shrugs and nods. He's willing to concede a shred. He flies at his machine again, doing a quick clean-up for a color job, and he drops the conversation. Sometimes I think "melting pot" is the wrong word. It's more like "salad dressing." After the violent shaking, the oil and the vinegar inevitably separate.

"Hey," Hank pipes up, "how about Pope Sitting Bull? That way the pope can put out the Bull Bull! Get it, the Bull Bull? Ya know, that's what they call press releases, papal bulls, or something..."

Oy, what can I do? Tecumseh! Leonard Peltier! Somebody give me some advice, something I can do in this crazyhouse of ink! Should I nail the bastards up on the cross-beams, or should I pour solvent over myself and beg them to throw a match? It's hard being an American, but a Jew, no less; an American *with* the Indians, a Jew *with* the Palestinians?

Guide to the Perplexed

The X of 1492

Columbus?

I leaf through the books, randomly skimming,
looking to discover Jews, not Columbus.

"In the same month
in which Their Majesties
issued the edict that
all Jews should be driven
out of the Kingdom
and its territories,
in the same month
they gave me the order
to undertake with sufficient
men my expedition of
discovery to the Indies."

Columbus, his diary.
Or, as they called
him in Spain, Cristobal Colon.
1492: the year of the Great Expedition;
and the year the Jews were expelled from Spain.

Jews again, even as America is hunted down.

1492: the year Spain is one, wed
by Their Catholic Majesties,
Ferdinand & Isabella.
Heathen Islam, after hundreds of years,
is driven out, gone.
I scratch my head, astonished:
Jews again, gone with the Arabs.
Spain was whole, Holy, Catholic, and
pure—and financially precarious.

With the Jews also went Spain's vehicle
for the passage of gold and trade,
as that was much of the role they played.

This was a bold step for Their Catholic Majesties.
Trade with Asia was essential, but the Arabs
had control of Palestine despite Holy Crusades,
while the Italians monopolized trade with the Arabs.
Spain and Portugal faced out, on the
cusp of the Mediterranean:
They sought another route.
Portugal surmised they could inch around Africa
to reach India—and they were closing in.

Enter pushy Columbus upon the Spanish Court
with his business scheme.
He could reach Asia via the West—
and take a sizeable cut of the profit
accrued from the seizure of the fabled
gold mines of Genghis Khan.

There was no question among scholars:
The world *was* round.
Too round in fact.
They computed that Columbus
would die of thirst
before reaching Asia.
How could they know
an entire hemisphere
stood in his path?
They cried objections.
But Spain was desperate, and risks
needed to be taken, especially
in regards to the grabbing of gold.
The Jews were expelled,
a whole civilization ejected.
The confiscated Jewish wealth
was used in part to finance
Columbus's enterprise.
How strange, even the first
to step ashore as the
Discoverer beached was a
merchant Jew, brought to
translate Oriental tongues:
unfortunately, he was
ignorant of Arawak.

Courtiers rumored that Cristobal
himself was a Jew.
Wasn't the leading Jewish
scholar of Italy named
Rabbi Joseph Colon?
How else could a mere son
of a weaver find such access
to the Royal Court
(and to the Royal Purse)?
Such mobility in feudal times
smelled suspiciously of Jew.
Perhaps the Inquisition missed
inquiring of such a one.
Perhaps it was just the hint
of what the voyage heralded—
a new world, a new class.
And, in its own way,
the expulsion of the Jews
heralded the same.

Columbus's fleet and the boats
of Jewish refugees fleeing East
all left from Palos harbor,
their wakes crossing,
a gigantic X
of the Jews and Columbus
crossing: X

as in X marks the spot
or the unknown of a vast algebra.
Two distinct and diverging directions,
a watery X washed over and dissolved.

The bows cross, and the Jews,
leaning against masts and railings,
wail at the last of Iberia.
Rabbi Jacob Habib of Salamanca,
may his memory be blessed,
prays, weeping.
He stares at his congregation
on the verge of delerium,

raises his arms to quiet them.
The boat sways, he glances
at the passing Santa Maria.
Only the boat creaks
in silence as the Rabbi speaks:

"It is so hard to leave home.
We lived well, not so poverty-stricken as those of Palermo,
despised by the Christians because they are all tattered
    and dirty
and forced to do hard labor with their hands at the King's
    incessant bidding;
nor were we so blessed as our brethren in Alexandria
who sit on rich rugs and drink raisin wine deep in study of
    the Torah.
Yes, we have transgressed to be cast so far, and we must
    look deep within for our sin.
We will find it fathomless,
though we have kept apart in the light of the Torah. . . .

"Mourn our dead, those who perished in the Arms of the Lord,
    killed by riot.
Myself, I mourn my sister Rachel and her children she sacrificed
    before God, the High & Exalted;
Rachel put her children next to her body, two on each side,
covering them with her two sleeves.
There they lay struggling in the agony of death,
and when the enemy seized the room they found her sitting
    & wailing over them—
'Show us the money that is under your sleeves,' they commanded.
But when it was the slaughtered children they saw,
they struck her & killed her,
& her spirit flew away & her soul found peace at last.

"I mourn them all, yet those who took their own lives,
    themselves dead
rather than to die at the hands of the unrighteous
they shall sit forever, basking in the light of the Lord,
with crowns of righteousness upon their heads. . . ."

The crowded deck of Jews
heaves up with cries.
Rabbi Jacob raises his head,
pointing to the three caravals of Colon:

"So there sails on that rumored Jew, Colon,
kept in the light of the King & Queen by his wild schemes.
I only hope that neither of us return.
Perhaps our mutual passing in our affliction is a sign
as once a rainbow stood as a sign.
We are cast to the sea,
spit out by our occupation of gold imposed by the state,
expelled by our steadfastness in the Law
the Lord Our God commands us to obey
& for which he sets apart our fate.
For what Christians and Our Lord demand of us
we receive such wealth of hatred.
So be it. We are chosen to be set adrift,
& through our suffering the whole world is uplifted.

"But this Colon, what of this Italian, this Jew?

"If he is one of us, his direction is opposite.
I think the rumor is not true.
We are forced to our money-lending, banned from other pursuits;
yet he embarks on his bold Enterprise by choice to loot
China, Sumatra, & all other Asian destinations.
He has cast himself to the sea, elected by his own gross
    ambition.

"We pass—my brethren, note this passing in our affliction.
Our wakes swamp over in conflicting directions.
We sail off to a new world holding fast to the ways of
    our fathers;
he to usurp the old.
Pray that we never return, but that by scorn & sacrifice
we endure as sheep in Abraham's fold.
Pray also that this Colon drowns,
dies of thirst & hunger with his crew,
never to port home with his calf of gold."

Salamanca's Rabbi Jacob Habib
implores Israel to remember
God is one.
Without hesitation, Colon sails on,
holds steadfast to his task
as stipulated by the Crown. . . .

Columbus? The myths on
elementary-school windows;
a man in tights with a telescope
staring off into eternity
as soldiers drive a cross
into a beach with Indians
keeping a cautious but curious
distance; him, the one
on the school window
after the turkey and Pilgrims
and those other Indians
come down? But how
did the initial step
mark the whole journey?

I turn the page, whereupon
enter Friar Bartolome de las Casas.
The Friar was there, saw the
expedition's success.
He was witness,
Jesus's servant sent to bless
Asiatics with mysteries
of Catholic holiness.
A reformer, he still sought
colonial possession,
but for years
he walked the Spanish Court
seeking adjustment of the
policy blazed by Columbus,
the policy of bestiality.
There he is now, stopping a
nobleman passing in the halls.
Breathless, the Friar

makes his appeal;
and by so doing hopes
to make his memory heal.

"I was there!

"I saw it, saw the Devastation of the Indies.

I chronicled that Cristobal, that whore Italian—
Viceroy of the Indies, Admiral of the Ocean Sea—
the titles so lately bestowed upon him.
No! Admiral of Death, Admiral of Mosquitoes!
I know. I saw it.
I went to preach the Cross—& I beheld again our Savior die.
Again His Life was sold for a measure of gold.

"Those gentle people came to greet us.
We towered like gods with our shields and swords.
In wonder & faith they made us welcome.
But Colon spied his prey early, whispering,
'That heathen, see, in his ear one gold pendant!
That one over there, seashells & gold around her neck are hung!'
Colon, his eyes grown wild, made his declaration:
This very isle was the secret gold mine of Genghis Khan
now under Spain's direction!

"Such playful jewelry, such little dabs of vanity
became the spark to light the fires of their misfortune.
With haste, he ordered Pacification.
Those newfound subjects who resisted burned
slowly over fires of green branches.
Shrieks & howls filled the air day & night.
The Admiral of Hell pitched arms & legs to his dogs
that prowled the hills so they could better
learn the taste for native flesh.
So horrible these screams that it became impossible to sleep,
& when I objected to the tumult
& for mercy made Holy plea,
he chose such nicety
as to gag his victims.
In silence they could weep.

"Certain this was the great Khan's secret mine, he made decree
that around their necks each of these unfortunates
must wear medallions to be notched at every appointed date
upon receipt of one whole measure of gold.
When the appointed day arrived his fearful subjects dutifully
    returned
with buckets of earrings, pendants, & other minor treasures,
and dutifully in turn Colon notched their coins & saved a few
    from being burned.

"But came the next date & fewer came with gold, mere flakes
    from streams.
Those that could not match the measure
instantly were dragged to the block, their hands severed.
Dismayed, they stared at chopped arms.

"This Admiral of Mosquitoes & Worms, this Plague,
could not see, would not believe what soon we learned.
Viceroy of Gnats! There was no more!
There was no gold on this isle, only a trinket's worth.
Yet this Admiral of the Ocean Sea
poured blood ceaselessly into that sad earth.
The truth left his madness undeterred.

"What tortures these poor people were cast;
to be made slave is enough,
yet more to be slave to the impossible task.

"I saw it.
As well I saw these people in such distress
that they rebelled
& fought steel swords with clubs & wood spears.
When revolt seemed hopeless mothers with awful tears
took the lives of their own children
so that by themselves choosing doom they held
a measure of dignity to their nation.

"A few years have gone, but in that meagre time
millions butchered.

My Lord, do you hear me? I know I speak long,
but stay so that you might stop this wrong.
Perhaps it didn't happen, only a friar's dream,
I pray—but my ears are filled with hideous screams.

"Cristobal Colon, Christopher!
Spain is amazed at his great new find.
They murmur he is kin to his namesake, St. Christopher,
who carried Our Lord Savior Jesus Christ
across the river on his back to save him from the flood.
They fancy this Christopher is also a ferryman of the Lord
as he carries blessings of Christ to new lands.
Oh yes, on his back he carries Christ's Body across the sea—
& there he dumps the carcass down for his dogs. . . .

I was there. I know.
I saw the Devastation of the Indies. . . ."

Slave of the Royal Treasury

A very good book, *The Jewish Question*. "Judaism," the author argues, "has survived not in spite of history, but by virtue of history. We must not start with religion in order to explain Jewish history; on the contrary, the preservation of the Jewish religion or nationality can be explained only by the 'real Jew,' that is to say, by the Jew in his economic and social role. . . .

"Whereas Catholicism expresses the interests of the landed nobility and of the feudal order, while Calvinism (or Puritanism) represents those of the bourgeoisie or capitalism, Judaism mirrors the interests of a precapitalist mercantile class. . . ."

Is this then the resolution, the underpinnings of the story: I have to dig deep into the working of the earth, not heaven, to recover who I am? I guess that's the first step, basic.

"The preservation of the Jews contains nothing of the miraculous."

Oh no, I'm beginning to slump in the chair, drowsy. This is no time to dream. Enough with this "Jewish Question"; I want the "Jewish Answer!" But I can't read on . . . after a day of work, the gnashing of machines . . . the kids screaming . . . the miraculous.

The miraculous? *No, the miraculous is the wrong part to drowse off on!* Enough poets have had dreams. It's old hat, a very ordinary thing at this point. Xanadu has been franchised out—you can see Xanadu at any freeway exit, waiting to accommodate. But it's no use, my head rolls off to one side. . . .

I see Jews scattered around the world, from Portugal's Lisbon to China's Kaifeng. The calendar flips pages just like an old movie. Even before Jesus or the Temple's last destruction, Jews scattered. The location—Palestine—was harsh, but ideal for cross-continental merchandising because it stood at the crotch of the Mediterranean. The Phoenicians showed how earlier, stretching from one end of the Mediterranean to the other. It was good business.

So in Europe you have Kings and the like after the Romans wasted away. They get serfs to work the land and nobles to work the serfs. And Jews? . . .

The camera moves across Europe, approaches the bend of the river from up above, closes in to the castle situated on the hilltop over the bend. Zooms into the courtyard, through the stone window to see one King hop from foot to foot, antsy:

"*Damn*, I want some silk or the like so I can display the style a King deserves . . . and some spice so the meat here don't smell so bad from castle mold . . . damn."

The Jester, always with an eye to the King's disposition, slides up with his usual advice. "King, what you need is *Jews!*"

"Huh? But they're not Christian, they're nasty."

"But, My Lord, explain then why the King of Worms hath some?"

"The King of Worms? Forsooth!"

The Jester does a little skip and leans on the throne. "It's like this, King. I heard it from Hans the Jester at Worms. You invite in some Jews, and they have connections and relatives all over. They can get silk and spice and those fancy turbans from India. They even associate with those crafty Arabs. They've been a tribe of merchants a long time and are hence well-versed. What's more, it's an endeavor a King should refrain from, seeing it's not noble like land is. . . . ."

The King smiles broadly, stamps his foot and bellows, "No King of Worms can outsilk me! *I want a Jew!*"

So the Jester hunts up a Jew, makes a small kickback deal on the side, and brings him to the King.

"My Lord," the Jew entreats, "have you ever seen such silk as I have shown you today for only 5 gold guilders given over to one such as myself who, in order to please Your Majesty, traveled so far to procure your dreams? And your Queen, My Lady, will respond, I am sure, with, 'Darling King, look at how stunningly this weave pleaseth the eye. Why don't you please the honor of this Hebrew merchant who brought this pleasure from so far, and by so doing, so please your Queen? . . .'"

The Queen says, "Ooo . . . indeed."

The King leans over to the Jester. "He speaks convincingly." Then he turns to the Jew. "The bargain is made, my honorable heathen subject."

Days later the king mopes. The Jester notices these things, so he comes up and says, "Perchance, why such melancholia, King?"

"Jester, now that the Queen enjoys these silks, where will I get all the gold to pay? Besides, I have a war in the works with that infernal King of Worms and I need money for that. There's not much gold in this serf business. . . ."

"King," the Jester lights up, "*you have another Jew Problem!*"

"Is that so?"

"Yes. You need to borrow some money, is that not so? Borrow from the Jew. Sure, he'll charge you interest. Usury is not befitting the likes of you—a Christian King of Christian land and Christian serfs—but it is well-deserved of the Jew, despicable as he is, a stranger with no land. He is so low he can't even be a serf. . . . "

"Surely." The King strokes his chin. "But how shall I make restitution of the loan?"

"Hearken, King. You started buying silk, and all the nobles go out and buy silk. The nobles have their estates, and they always itch to weaken yours, right? They're borrowing from the Jew already, and here you are moping. But hearken. The Jew is allowed here only by your say so, right?"

King puffs up, "By my Royal Dispensation."

"Well, he can only get into this money-lending business on your say so, right? (Anyway, you're not going to allow the heathen to do anything else anyway.) So. Everytime he gets back a loan—say with good 50% interest—you take a cut. How about you take 10%? That way when those craven nobles pay back the coins, it's coins in *your* purse."

"Excellent, Jester, excellent. Who'll believe us, though?"

"Easy. You promise to protect the Jew. The nobles won't carp too much, because they crave the filthy lucre, and you declare the Jew officially to be 'Slave of the Royal Treasury.' That's what the King of Worms decreed.

"Sure, that way you're not doing ungodly undignified money lending, but you're raking in the coin anyway."

"I like it . . . *Slave of the Royal Treasury . . . my Jew. . . .* "

"Ah, but here's the catch of the catch, My Lord. The Prince of Padua hath trod this path before. The nobles are liable to wax irritable over this after they start building up some heavy debts. You yourself just might get over your own head, if I may be so bold . . . I mean with a war and all. Also, some of those Counts and Dukes are wont to go astray in their debauchery, and the Jew will move to take their land for payment—"

"*Alack, a Jew with land?*" The King grabs for his sword.

"Hold it, King. Here's how we operate. The Jew is Slave of the Royal Treasury, right? When they exceed their welcome, simply kill them off, throw out the rest, tear up the notes, and confiscate everything they own. The remainder move out to some other King, and you're whole, Holy, Catholic, and pure."

"Assured, a most wise policy. But what happens when I need some more money?"

"After things settle some and the nobles are back in line—you call back your faithful slave. Now you extend this invitation, but only after your faithful slave pays some big fees and honorariums for the honor to be once more your slave. This way you get your slave to pay his way back into slavery—and you're swelling with gold both coming and going. True, My Lord?"

"True, dear Jester. Slave of the Royal Treasury . . . *my* Jew."

I wake from this dream, sticky and slightly nauseous. A movie musical comedy version of history? The cartoon truth? *The Miraculous, the Ridiculous, and the Real?* "Judaism has survived not in spite of history, but by virtue of history." A crack, a necessary anomaly, in the history of feudalism? A meandering past King Solomon and his Temple built by his Jewish slaves, past Moses fleeing the lash, in and out of classes. Ach. "The 'real Jew', that is to say, the Jew in his economic and social role. . . ." The 'real' Maccabees? the economic and social role of Treblinka?

We weren't suddenly blasted out of the Middle Ages. Beyond the Slave, a *people* grew, a story.

I have a hard time focusing my eyes again as I stand in front of my mirror, rubbing my eyes, pinching my cheek, slowly yanking my nose.

"The Slave of the Royal Treasury? *His* Jew?"

Guide to the Perplexed

The story of the People is more than
the Slave of the Royal Treasury can tell.
The story grows
beyond 1492, enlarging from long before,
becomes a guide, is the People.
The People live because of memory.
You, remember now, and by remembrance
bind yourself to the story;
bind the memory to your forehead
so it dangles continually before your eyes,
through which the world is seen,
witnessed,
and changed.

Long ago the People were wanderers.
Alongside their sheep they roamed, thankful.
Then they were captured as they visited
the Nile River People to seek relief from famine.
The People were put to the lash
as the Slave-Master King demanded bricks mixed
with their blood for great buildings.
Until Moses, burning and stuttering, led them beyond
the warriors through swamps and into
the desert that was freedom.
The People left, they wandered again, tribes
bound together by a way to live.
Moses tore out a purpose from hard rock.
A mountain trembled over their heads.
The People saw a wholeness, a oneness,
and this was their bond.

With this bond they seized rich land
from the farmers of Canaan,
themselves beginning to farm.
No longer adrift, they cultivated their honey and milk.
Their crops came from Mother Earth, were attached.
But the oneness came from outside, beyond, throughout.
The oneness was not attached, was a father.

39

This set the People apart from the others.
All the others knew their own mother!
But the more wheat grown, the more flocks multiplied,
the more the Patriarch became the oneness
alone, not Mother.
And so with abundance came owning.
The tribes had chiefs, they had their farms, their sheep.
They had their stories of how the world came to be,
how flood washed over it.
Oneness was a flood, if it wished, frightful
yet sympathetic, refracted through droplets of mist
as colors of a promise for which the People
climbed up high places to seek, thankful.
No longer roaming ones, simple and lean, the People
prospered with wheat, for which they were
grateful to the oneness reflected in themselves.
They became more like other farmers,
more like the Nile River People even.
Eventually some called for a King
to gather all the tribes around.
This was new, to become like the Nile River People
who had kept them in bondage before.
Yet they chose,
because oneness was becoming complex, split.

The People divided into the owners and the owned.
Slaves built great buildings with their blood for the King.
Prophets breathed in the oneness, stood out of their bodies
to see it, to see what was becoming, how the bond loosened.
They went up to where hot springs bubbled.
The madmen bathed themselves, sweating,
then they threw themselves into cool streams
as icy water pounded through them, and they cried,
"Justice rushes out between the rocks, ineffable
and constant, refracted as a promise.
This is our bond! Wash your body in it!
AAAAAAAAAARRRRRRRRRRRRRGGGGGGGGGHHHHHHHHHHH!"
It wasn't that the Prophets could see the future.
They cried out to keep the People whole
by Justice, despite Solomon's wisdom of conquest.

Their past tore out a purpose from hard rock.
Others began to attack the people in turn,
even as the realm of their Slave-Master Kings magnified.
Other roaming people, other farmers, other
slave-master realms, all had to fight off
mighty empires as well as one another.
More and more the world divided into the owners and the owned.

The Prophets reminded the People of their bond,
the story of deliverance, of freedom.
Justice reflected oneness in droplets of blood.
Doomed, the People kept themselves despite empires.
Knowing who they were, they rebelled against conquerers.
Though lost, they demanded themselves,
even as the rich among them were
carted off to exile, captive again, or even
as they returned to impose themselves again on the poor
left behind as negligible remnants.
The People were caught in cross-currents
in which they roamed again, not with
flocks but with merchandise, crossing
between hunter people, the farmers, the shepherds,
and the other city-dwellers of the empires.
Later, when the great buildings of the Romans were
sacked by the wild nomad tribes, the People
kept the far-flung reaches of the world bound
by their constant traffic and trade.
Their Kingdom itself was destroyed, their Temple ruined.
Yet the story and the promise had become the People.
No longer was the story bound to the People;
now the People were bound to the story.
Without the memory the People would disappear;
the story grew greater than the People themselves,
dislodged, drifted freely among the nations,
and still the People clung to it, required it,
became droplets scattered across the earth
to replenish the memory.
They were the People of the Book.
Once they were tribes, then a Slave-Master nation.
A people scattered across time, across Europe

and the Mediterranean, they had become a bond,
ineffable and constant, a code,
a transcription of loving-kindness,
an obligation chosen, a belief more real by the change.
Now religion held the throne of Jerusalem;
the Sabbath ran border outposts facing strange lands.

The People came to the lands of Europe
where Landlord Kings drew their lives from the farmers.
The farmers were attached to their land,
chained to their plows, secured to the father
who sat in his big stone house.
It would be that way forever,
because Jesus died in Jerusalem.
The Holy Men said this world was natural.
The Landlord Kings agreed, assigning
the Slave of the Royal Treasury
between the owners and the owned
in the ascending order of things.
The Slave traded money and goods,
adding to what was already natural,
and just as naturally he was killed.
The Slave—despised, prosperous, protected,
terrorized, all in turn—was nothing
without the Royal Treasury.
The Slave, attached to the King, was wealthy;
but most of the People were poor,
artisans or laborers, keeping to the day of rest,
guarding the bond of their exile.

Then came those who were not Kings;
they bought work and sold its value,
uprooted money and replanted profit.
They owned tools, not the land,
and they rented workers of tools
while they sat in big stone cities.
They were busy, tossing the world into the air,
bossing over those they rented.
They were the Busy Ones.
Market was natural, Holy Men said,

because a spirit walked in Jerusalem.
The Busy Ones wrote a newer testament: *cash*.
The Slave, designated handler of money,
was poor competition, attached
as he was to the old Landlord King.
The Slave was outmoded.
Once he was foreign but essential,
but now he was not just strange, he was irrelevant.
Grown strong, the Busy Ones told
the Landlord Kings, "Throw the Slave out!"
They were now to be masters of *all* Busyness.
And soon they were gone from all
the countries of the Western sunset.
England: *out!* France: *out!* Spain: *out!*
And the Slave left, taking all the rest.

With their oneness the People
stood under a splendid canopy of stars.
Despite the pain, the People held
a belief more real by the change.
Drifting again, the world was their tent,
but this desert was not freedom,
only a place that was safe:
They went to Poland.
There the farmers tilled their plots
while the Landlord King gave them anchor.
The Busy Ones had not come so far;
this world stayed calm
to which the Slave and his People attached.
The Slave was welcomed, the artisans
given tasks, and the People thrived in towns
washed on all sides by a sea of serfs.
They spoke their own tongue, interpreted
their own Law in Council, told the story.
Yet, though the Busy Ones had not come,
Poland did not stay strong for very long;
it began to rot, bringing devastation.
The bloodthirsty Horse people drove
across the land, as did the Swede,
causing sadness and death for years.

Finally three empires tore the proud Eagle apart
as the lords and farmers and the people wept.
A wing to Prussia, the other to Austria,
and the heart to the Mad Bear, Russia.

Defeat was laid to the strange People
who kept to their oneness despite
the sad trinity that was now their land.
The People faced nothing but poverty and ruin.
The Slave of the Royal Treasury,
the great moneylender and merchant,
became nothing but a peddler with a pushcart,
a shadow of his former self.
This did not lessen the hatred
of the "natives" for their "guests."
Many of the People, attached to the lords,
were used by them to do their dirty work:
somebody was needed to collect
taxes off the half-dead serfs.
And the serfs began to hate this middleman
with a venom that only increased
as the crisis deepened.
The People were not blessed,
anointed and bathed in the waters
of the church, as was the nobleman
who far more deserved the curse.
Overtaxed and overworked and underfed,
the peasants rose up and . . . killed Jews.

Finally, even the Busy Ones reached Poland.
They tossed grief into the air,
using blood to fuel manufacture.
The ex-serf–now-worker toiled
in the mines, the railroads, the big mills.
The People were banned from such pursuits,
confined to an ever-narrowing realm
of small-craftsmen, middlemen,
and workers in light industries.
The Jew was no longer the foreign sand
around which the pearl of the world
of the lords and ladies formed.

Poverty grew deeper;
the hooligans likewise grew crazier,
and the hatred for the People
became a religious cult.
The Busy Ones, helped by the Landlord Kings,
saw that this was good—for them.
The Mad Bear's Landlord Czar
stirred the brew with great deliberation
so peasants and workers would not notice
his own hands around their throats.
The People were stuck between
the anvil of the landlords
and the hammer of Busyness.
Naturally, they were crushed.

What choices did the People have?
Where was Moses, burning and stuttering?
What could they do?
Some cried, "Go, seek refuge
in strange lands—go to the *Goldeneh Medina,*
go to America!" And millions did.

Others wailed, "Await the Messiah
who will uplift the House of David
and set once again the King
upon his throne in Jerusalem!"
But it was religion that held the throne,
not the Slave-Master Kings.
They prayed, transporting themselves
in ecstasy to the presence of oneness
in sheer mystic piety. They
suffered and saw God. They danced and
saw God. They died and
saw God.

Some agitated for the metaphysical lure
of Zion in the realm of politics.
"We shall be normal like the others!
The nation shall be restored in Palestine!"
Perhaps it sounded plausible in their pain.
By then the Europeans had swept the world,

planting themselves among peoples
to grow as new crops in the image of home;
and though the People were strangers in Europe,
Europe was the home they took to Zion.
They would do the same, planting Jews
to contain the vines of Arab peoples.
They became the foreign sand
around which the pearl of empire formed—
first British, then American—and they enjoyed
the enmity of Arabs cast out from their own homes.
Some went, hardly the amount that found
refuge in the Zion of America,
but many cherished the fantasy.

Others shouted out, "Neither
feudalism nor capitalism
can make us free—only socialism.
Since the Revolution in France
we have been bound to the commandments
of equality and revolt,
instructing us to fight
the blood of centuries of hate
built on the rotting corpse of Europe!
Only by the struggle of all people
to rid humanity of class rule
can we, trapped in cruel fashion
by class society, smashed
between the anvil of feudalism
and the hammer of capitalism,
can we—"
They fought, ultimately throwing themselves
against the inexorable bestiality of the Reich.

Unrelenting, the People moved across
the face of Europe's history
as history, equally unrelenting, met them—
September 1, 1939—with death.
"We are marching to Warsaw to beat up Jews,"
the Nazi troops sang.
Nazism burned, the ugly X

of crazed capitalism; and Hitler
became so monumental an evil
he reached Biblical proportions.
The hammer and the anvil;
the heavy hammer crashing against cold anvil,
pounding—until . . .
only the voices of the dead can be heard,
dead fighters of the Warsaw Ghetto, of Treblinka,
heard across blankness:
"We died because we were already dead.
The question for us became not one of survival
but of how to die:
rebellion became a document for others to read
and we wrote it in the streets of the Ghetto, fighting.
You are in America, another story grown from ours.
The question for you, child,
is how you live.
Not in guilt, not in sorrow or vengeance;
but to continue, to move your hand with ours,
to resolve the contradictions we describe in our death
in favor of life."

The heavy hammer crashing against cold anvil,
pounding, until . . .
What would *I* have done then?
My family, each in their way, made their choice,
most perished:
Rutka and Marek to Tel Aviv;
a few to America;
my father's father praying as they turned on the gas;
my communist cousins fighting, fleeing to the Soviet zone
only to be mistaken for spies and shot;
and then there's Rosa with scars on her arms and legs,
and the incessant stories filled with such
horror and luck that even she can't believe them.

What will I do now?
I bind the memory for a sign to my fist:
the story of a people, only one.
Long ago they were wanderers alongside their sheep;

they saw themselves in droplets of mist, a promise.
The tribes had become a Slave-Master nation
that had become a bond; a Slave
that became a caste, a People
who burned in Europe
to become a document
fighting in the streets.
Still, the People are divided, split;
the document has not yet resolved
in favor of life.

By remembrance I bind myself to the story,
and in myself are traces of it, the small
direct experiences of one life, even as it
dangles blindly before my eyes.
The Story is incomplete without the evidence,
without my own investigation;
I need to take inventory,
to take stock, item by item:
    Nazis who said we were indigestible to
    the belly of Europe . . .
    Arabs who now are indigestible to
    the belly of Israel . . .
    wings of the F-15s over Palestinian camps . . .
    the Negev of tanks . . .
    America this strange land we
    wander seeking Justice,
    shouting, "AAAAAARRRRRRRRRGGGGGGGGGGHHHHHHHHH!"

The story of the People is more than
we can tell, a story that grows
beyond 1948, enlarging from long before,
a story felt bit by bit, itemized
in the small experiences of one life,
still to be investigated, sought,
Justice reflecting oneness in droplets of blood,
so the story can become a guide, be the People.
Through the memory the world is seen:
We witness it,
We change:

My Messiah Is in My Hands and My Homeland Is Where I Fight

I Will Never Shake Hands with the Enemy
of My Homeland

1962

My mother's father was a patriot, one of the highest Jews in the
    Polish government.
My mother spoke with pride, *"He was a decent man."*
For years just what his post was remained a mystery to me.
When the Nazis invaded Poland his hair turned stark grey overnight.
The Nazi officer entered his office to take charge & extended his hand:

"Because Poland is conquered it does not mean we cannot behave like
    gentlemen,"
& he clicked his heels.

The Jewish bureaucrat kept his hand to his side.
"I will never shake hands with the enemy of my homeland."

Shortly thereafter he died of a mysterious ailment.
Did the doctor give him the "wrong" medicine, or did he die
    at the hands of the Germans?

His photograph used to preside on the piano as I played mazurkas.
He sat by his desk, the plaque of Pilsudski staring from the wall,
    his noble hands folded next to a gilded telephone, his eyes so
    liquid a blue
they were two transparent Baltics even in the black & white.
He looks very decent sitting behind his desk.
Like me, he could pass for goy.

I chop at my Junior High School mazurkas on the piano & wonder:

Why can't *I* act with restraint, dignity, & quiet fortitude?
Why do I have to buy a ticket at Yom Kippur to atone for
    my sins?
Why does Lucille Ball act with such disrespect, so brash,
    so embarrassing?

Why do these middle class homes look like Zsa Zsa Gabor's
    eyelids?
Why do these Americans rail against the black ones?
Why is it when the Italian kids curse the Jews I pale but
    keep my secret?

I dream of a Poland where valiant horsemen throw themselves
    desperately against Nazi tanks.
Of course, the Polish anti-Semites throw Jewish college students out
    of 5th-floor windows—
"Out! Out! No Jews in Physics!"
—but my dreams rode in the cavalry & half of my heart passed
    for goy:
"Hello, I am Count Hilton Manfred Obenzinger . . .
I will never shake hands with the enemy of my homeland."
Like him, I could easily pass for goy.

1965

Later, I enter Columbia College, aching to knit brows in cafes
over great questions of Contemporary Civilization,
    humble to sit amongst giants.
As if by sinister plan, the University places me in the
    same dorm room
with the son of Polish Catholic peasants on football scholarship.
Why is it Svojewlewski & Obenzinger don't get along?
Both our names torture WASP tongues equally.
I from Polish Jewish petty-bourgeoisie & he from Polish
    Catholic peasantry;
he aspires to Business School & I to Marxist beatnik poetry.
Why is it I am anti-War & he is pro?
Why do we both scramble to be class traitors?
Is there secret meaning in the fact that the University Alma Mater
is the same tune as Deutschland Uber Alles?
Deep in fraternities the Tweeds sing,

    "Oh, Harvard's run by millionaires
    And Yale is run by booze,
    Cornell is run by farmer's sons,
    Columbia's run by Jews . . ."

Yet no one throws me out the 5th-floor window.
It's a ditty sung far from my ears as this Jew contemplates
   Contemporary Civilization,
as another writes deep neo-Talmudic theses entitled *The Meaning*
   of Meaninglessness,
while yet another fans rebellion on the verge of Harlem.
Uneasy, Obenzinger & Svojewlewski co-exist in America,
Americans like it or not—
the evidence of the pain of Poland
locked in dormitory bunk beds on Broadway.

1967

Finally, I return to Poland to take up the mantle of my grandfather.
With long hair of 1967 & American LSD, I take my place amongst
my long-lost countrymen.
Born in Brooklyn, I have come to the Cafes of Warsaw
to announce the resurrection of the Yiddisheh Polack.
I stick my thumb out by the road in the rolling woodland.

Hardly a car goes by as I stand on one end of a bridge on the
   banks of a fat green river.
A dusty village stretches out opposite me, & along the riverbank
ruins of an enormous church sit next to a wide WW II bombcrater,
   overgrown & weedy.
Peasants drive carts laden with vegetables to the market.
A grandma sweeps the bridge slowly with a broom.
An old peasant walks up the road; he stops a foot in front of my
   face, squinting.

"Hello, good morning," I say in creaky Polish, smiling.

He stares, squints again & replies, *"So what?"*

"I'm American."

"So what?

"How are you? I hope you're feeling well."

"So what?"

"I'm very well, thank you." I began to panic, my Polish running low.

"So what?" he stares. *Maybe he thinks I'm Jewish,* I think.

"I'm American, I don't speak Polish much, but my parents came
    from Poland."

His eyebrow lifts a bit. *"So what?"* he reasserts, stares,
    squints at my long hair,
& finally spits, then walks on across the bridge.

Maybe he thinks I'm Jewish. . . .

Dropped off in Krakow I walk lost,
trying to find my way out to the road.
Finally I stumble across a sleepy tourist office.
A young blonde boy, a student of English, directs me,
even accompanies me through Medieval streets.
"Say, do you listen to music?" he asks.
"Yes, I do—what do you mean?—I enjoy Chopin very much
& want to see his birthplace."
I'm very pleased at my international etiquette & respect for
    Polish culture.
I look up at the ancient parapets of Krakow, the university
    students
racing through narrow streets.
The Polish eagle waves on my caparison.
"No, I mean, I listen to Radio Luxembourg.
I like "I'm Going to San Francisco with Flowers in My Hair."
It's the number one hit. I'd like to go to California someday,
see the Beachboys."

I stop short, dumbfounded in Krakow,
"Oh yeah . . . California . . . flowers . . . Beachboys . . . yeah."

"Here's the bus stop now. Well, good luck. Maybe I'll be seeing
  you again," he smiles, winks, & adds,

"Let me shake your hand," then extends his hand.

I shake it & thank him. He walks away, humming.

I click my heels. . . .

Brave People

He tells me about the "Brave People"—Mojave—his own
as we round a bend, the car rattling up Rt. 17
where Oakland drops down from the hills to the Bay:

    "When they got their arm shot by the enemy
    they just slap some mud"—*thwap* on his arm—
    "& keep on walking maybe 40 miles in one night
    across desert. Just like that"—*thwap*—
    "Damn! Those people were something.
    The Brave People was what they called them.
    They walk 40 miles to beat back the Spanish,
    defeat them too, but then they let
    the Americans come in from behind."

He laughs at the story and tells me more:
Yes, the Creator made many things & many people.
Among these, what about the white one, what of him?
Everyone went about their business except him.
He went his own way, a fuckup, dropped out of sight
    into a hole
to live underground.
Imagine what Mojave thought when the white man
    reapppeared:

Aiiee! They came out of the cracks in rocks!
So pale, so hidden from sun!

Yes We Have No Bananas

"Yes, we have no bananas."
That's what they sang as my father clung
to the rails of the steam ship
pale from the depths of steerage.
Ellis Island has no bananas?
No bananas in this, the Goldeneh Medina?

In Lublin he wanders through the woods
with his friends to picnic.
Pounced upon by thugs—*"Jews!*
Out of our woods, you dirty Jews!"—
they were chased back towards the ghetto
until he grabs some acorns, fires
them back, cracks some heads:
"I'll teach you to beat on Jews!"

"Yes, we have no bananas"
was what they sang
on the Lower East Side.
"Apple pie & coffee" was all the English he knew.
"Apple pie & coffee," he said
& others they laugh, these Americans,
they call him a *"greenhorn,"*
& they sing *"Yes,*
we have no bananas,"
as he wanders the garment district
looking for work,
eating apple pie & coffee
day after day in the automat.

Behind the Redwood Curtain

The Indian tilts his head towards the new bridge spanning
    Humboldt Bay,
connecting giant pulp mills of Manila & Samoa—
odd names for scrappy sand-dune towns of poor white shacks—
as we sit in the Eureka Cafe, nursing coffee.
"Bridge goes over a island, Indian Island they call it.
They massacred a whole village there in a rampage"—

> "... neither age nor sex had been spared. Little children
> and old women were mercilessly stabbed and their skulls
> crushed with axes. When the bodies were landed at Arcata,
> a more shocking and revolting spectacle never was exhibited
> to the eyes of a Christian and civilized people...."

I look in the direction, but only see ghosts in dense fog
& smell the sharp sweet pulp smell of the mills.
"They got it for a freeway to the pulpmills
but ecologis' want it for the birds—we want it for ourselves
and the birds, for our cultural center...."

"So, you gonna *take* it?" I exclaim.

"*Shh,*" he hushes me up. "Where you think you are, SF?
You got to watch what you say here.
Someone from Straight Arrow vigilante might hear you,
& you might end up mysterious dead in the woods.
They don't like Indians, ecologis', or the likes of you."

My Indian friend chuckles, "Well, this is what we call
living behind the 'Redwood Curtain'...."

> The pro-Indian reporter who condemned the slaughter for the
> Arcata *Northern Californian* became the target of vigilantes ...
> "*No one seems to know who was engaged in the slaughter but it
> is supposed to have been....*" For that indiscretion of outrage,
> Bret Harte—cub reporter, original "local color" gold-rush story-
> teller, secret Jew—was outcast, run out of town by the lynch mob.

The loggers across from us look hardy & peaceful,
just working people eating breakfast.
The sweet sickening pulp fog drifts across Manila.
Our white companion leans over, "Sure, you need to be careful.
We're working with the Okies at Manila, they come for the
    logging & the mills
& they stay at the bottom along with Portuguese.
We got an agreement I guess:
They don't preach God & we don't preach Marx,
together we fight.
Maybe they can see what's right for the Indians too.
But we gotta be careful."

Strange, this California, like flypaper
sticking Manila Okies Portuguese Injuns
Jews
on the same sheet.

"This is what you call
living behind the 'Redwood Curtain' . . . ha!"

Anyway, Isn't California Enough?

A friend in San Francisco receives a letter.

"Hey, listen to this, just listen to this," he demands. He reads it out loud:

Dear _____,

I am writing to tell you that your Auntie Sarah died last week. The cancer was a long time advancing and, we hope, she was well prepared.

I don't know if you are blessed with sentimentality, but I and your aunt talked about you the night before she died. Now that your parents have passed away as they have, there are few relatives of yours who would concern themselves with your welfare. Blood is thick, they say, but I have to tell you that our conversation did not add one bit to her peace of mind those last moments on earth.

Your disgusting love for the Arabs is too much to bear. I don't know what your parents did to deserve a punishment like you. You have deserted your people and become a misguided 'humanist' instead of being a Zionist and standing up for your people. Your own people you treat like dirt to throw at the Arabs. Your behavior pained your aunt greatly, and you should only remember it to feel ashamed what you do to your people, what you did to her! Someday we might be able to talk when you have taken your rightful position as a defender of your people. Until then I wish you stay well as I wish any fly or bug or insect as long a life as they deserve. Just don't crawl back to your family.

Your Disappointed Uncle

My friend sighs, drops the letter down: "Thousands of years . . . they sure got expert on how to make you feel guilty. I feel like shit."

"So, you gonna make your *aliyah* to Israel? Gonna emigrate?

"No, of course not. *Anyway, isn't California enough?*"

My Messiah Is in My Hands and My Homeland Is Where I Fight

Yet a forerunner comes to the defense of outcasts. He speaks in a dark-lit tailor's shop, piles of pants and vests and dresses all about him clustered like disciples. A friend of his has stepped into his shop— maybe it's 1919 or it's 1929—to discuss a proposal. An honest friend, equal in honesty to the tailor; and the tailor responds, casting the cuff in his hands aside, with earnest casual flick. . . .

"My heart did not remain silent within me
over the blood of my brothers being spilled in Bialystok . . .
I was restless because of the pogroms.
Mama, Papa, my sisters and their children, did they live?
I hadn't heard a word from them since the pogrom
and didn't know if they lived.
Only from my wife and our darling boy did I hear,
and they came over to America to safety—and more starvation.

"Still, I am ashamed I left.
If I had known what was going to happen here,
I would not have gone to America.
I myself agitated that one should not leave for America
but stay and fight against the Czar until we were victorious.
(And we did win, at the cost of so much blood!)
Now I feel like a liar and a coward.
I agitated my friends, placed them in the danger of soldiers'
    guns and bullets.
And I myself ran away. . . .

"I was drafted to the Czar's cavalry,
and there I once hit my superior.
The military court was about to sentence me,
and I fled at three o'clock in the morning.
I gave my gun and sword to the revolutionaries,
and they gave me passage money to America.
But that was not the end of it.
What did I run away to except more starvation and degradation?
One went about with strong hands those days.

One wanted to sell them for a bit of bread to feed
the little one, and no one wants to buy.
They tell you cold-bloodedly: 'We don't need you.'
Can you imagine how heartsick one gets?

"I didn't come here for a fortune, but where was bread?
God forbid you should find a job outside
the needle trades or other jobs the Jews are allowed.
The goyisheh workers would hound you off the job.
And then to work, as gladly I did, was such torture
in sweatshops, putting out collars and pants.
Old men walked from shop to shop
with their sewing machines strapped to their backs.
Even as young men they were bent double by the weight
and the bending over when they did find work.
They grew old—and bent almost down to the ground.

"Seymour, you remember the song . . .

> 'To me there came a cousin,
> Pretty as gold was she, the greenhorn.
> Cheeks like pomegranates,
> Feet that just wanted to dance.'

"Yes, I had a cousin like so, as did you,
teeth like pearls, hair like silk,
but she came to America to sew the shirts and the pants
day after day just not to starve . . .

> '. . . And so passed the years:
> My cousin became a ruin.
> She gathered paychecks week by week
> Until nothing was left of her.

> 'Today, when I meet my cousin
> And I ask her: "How you doing, greenhorn?"
> She sighs and I read from her expression:
> "Columbus' land should only burn!"

'"Brenen zol Columbus' Medina!"'

"I work and I work in Columbus' land.
Finally I found my niche as a tailor,

not itinerant with the Singer on the back
but with a little shop, there to do my work year after year.

"Still, I am ashamed I left Bialystok.
And I mourn those that died behind.
But now, now you speak to me about the Friends of Zion
and settlements in Palestine
and return to a homeland you say is mine.

"You ask me in the name of socialism and all I love.
Shall this be socialism reserved only for the Jew,
and the Arab excluded although we remain in numbers few?
Shall we hunt like the Mormons for our land?
And, like the Indian, is it the gun we hope the Arab understands?
Already two colonies of Jews in South Dakota have failed,
and I wonder how much to the Mormon the comparison holds true.

"Sure, go back to build the Temple anew,
to pray, to remember the martyrs of Masada and the others.
But for years we did not return to rebuild the Kingdom of our Fathers,
and Sabbatai Zevi was shown to be false prophet long ago.
My Messiah is in my hands, and my homeland is where I fight.

"All my life I stayed ashamed, told no one
until I tell you now that once I fled
and left so many behind for dead.
This Jew doesn't need a big head
filled with hopeless dreams
of stolen Arab fig-trees, Arab flocks, and Arab streams.

"And if your dream does come true, I ask only that you see
who it is that suffers, and whether payment
will be asked years hence for such theft and hostility.

"I know you have suffered too, and you mean no harm,
but as for me, the answer is *No.*

"No.

"Ashamed, I left once, but to be ashamed again
to leave and even yet ashamed to come,
is more shame than I want to know.

"Seymour, pass me that gabardine by your arm . . ."

I'm a Yurok Indian & I'm Proud & You Can Take Your Goddam White Man's Religion Back Over the Ocean Where It Came from & Shove It

He tipped the Oly up to the blue
& polished it off.
I steered the beat up Caddy
away from ruts & he
flung the can out the window
into a confusion of manzanita & oak & second growth

"Ya know why I did that?"
he asked like a bark.
"Uh no, why?"
"Cause this is *my* land
& I can do any goddam thing I *want*
on *my* land!"
& then his anger subsided.

What's his he'll take, unashamed, like
spotlight a deer, blind it & blow it away.
"Yer a printer. Print me
a bumper sticker says:

I'M A YUROK INDIAN & I'M PROUD
& YOU CAN TAKE YOUR GODDAM WHITE MAN'S RELIGION
BACK OVER THE OCEAN WHERE IT CAME FROM
& SHOVE IT!"

Sometimes anger & hope & shame spun together
can get longer than a 65 Caddy bumper.
He's been saying the same things for years.
It explodes, tears through imported Scottish weed
& Himalaya berries, goes crazy.
Original redwood has been cleared for
long rows of sublets in San Jose
& the 2nd growth is unruly & a tangle.

Being white & in endless supply
I need to check my own panic
or my own paternal winks.
He don't know all the answers
except his—
& even those don't come with instructions
on how to assemble
an authentic model of a nation.

He's been saying it for years:
"We are the evidence of this
Western Hemisphere."
We swerve down the road, him
pulling out his 38
taking pot shots at beehives
& laughing it up.

The So-Called Jew

A Zionist sympathizer raises his hand for a question.

"I want to direct my question to the so-called Jew that spoke earlier. How can you possibly say that Zionism is the same as racism? I was very disturbed at all the things you were saying, but—this! I'm hurt and angry. I've worked to support the civil rights movement, I've sat as a member of multi-cultural committees here at SF State, and I can't understand that at all. Israel is a democracy, the light, a beacon for all the world's oppressed, I can't—"

"I'm the 'so-called Jew,' and I'd like to answer," I interrupt. Earlier the Palestinian students had explained their position with a great deal of restraint mixed with pain and passion and with unremitting logic. Jewish Zionists in the audience hissed and asked loaded questions, goading the Arabs. I had spoken, confusing the hecklers into silence, they not quite sure how to deal with this "so-called Jew." For that matter, neither was I so sure of how to cope with them. I hoped, at least, that I wouldn't be shot.

"Zionism is the call for *all* Jews to in-gather upon the land of Palestine with the understanding that anti-Semitism is a permanent feature of life—"

"That's right!"

"—and, as a result, the only solution to anti-Semitism is this in-gathering and the formation of an *exclusively* Jewish state. Along with this in-gathering there's the 'out-dispersal' of the Palestinians, Moslem and Christian, already living on the land. Zionism has made an *exclusively* Jewish state. This means that Jews have power, and everyone else—Palestinians—has none. It's a lot like the way the white South African apartheid system treats black Africans. Israeli policy has been aimed above all towards taking Arab land and kicking out the people. What else is going on with plans to build more and more settlements in the West Bank? That's what people mean when they say that Zionism is a form of racism.

"Besides that, too, Arab and non-white Jews face a lot of discrimination. It seems things are set up to benefit European Jews mainly. . . .

"Anyway, it's strange, this thing about 'anti-Semitism is permanent,' something that will never change. Think about it. Was this true in the days of King Solomon's empire? Or in the days when Persia liberated Jewish exiles in Babylon? Is *anything* permanent? Even if I completely rejected the religious notions of Judaism, there are still groups that would still, no matter what I said, insist I was, and I always would be, a Jew: Zionists and Nazis! Think about that! A strange thing, this 'permanence'; it brings together such unlikely bed-fellows."

The Zionists in the audience smirk and hiss.

"OK," I persist, "has the existence of the state of Israel really helped fight anti-Semitism? Zionists have always been more inter-ested in getting immigrants than in fighting anti-Semitism where Jews already live. Do you think promoting colonialism helps in dealing with anti-Semitism among Arabs and other Third World people? Is-rael, buttressed by the United States, staunch friend of South Africa, Somoza, of every disgusting regime in the world—*this* combats anti-Semitism? Israel speaks in our name?

"I know this is hard to comprehend, because of all the suffering that Jewish people have been through, all the racism, the death. But here we are: the oppressed themselves have become the oppressors. In-credible! I have a hard time dealing with *that....*"

Something very hard to comprehend. *The oppressed themselves have become the oppressors!* But it was such a vision, a desperate hope. I can see in their faces something to believe out of which sense can be molded. I felt that tug too. I wasn't immune, even as I sat in the music room listening to Yiddish records in the Jewish Community Library, thumbing through old Zionist texts. Golda Meir smiled from a photo on the wall—such a grandma.

I leafed through a book published in 1947, the year I was born, a paean to the ideas of Zionism. The graphics were beautiful: a face of an inspired young woman in khaki, joyous kibbutzim, elderly gentle-men tilling the soil with the caption "Intellectual Peasants." I was struck that I was born on the eve of the birth of the Jewish State, and its existence dodged my life. There, in these pages, shone forth the whole progressive or socialist rationale for Zionism; I studied it:

Herzl's theory of Zionism was fundamentally bourgeois in its con-ception—but Jewish immigrants into Palestine came largely from the lower classes of Eastern Europe, and were strongly subject to Socialist ideas.

The link was fashioned by a Russian-Jewish theoretician, Ber Borochov, who for the first time expressed the idea of Socialist Zion-ism. His ideas showed a marked parallelism with Herzl's visions, though his starting point was quite different. He stated that the Jews in their forced role as petty bourgeois, or as employed in the last stages of production only, lacked the strategic basis for a class struggle and could never build up a real socialist movement. In order to remedy their shortcoming, the Jews had to create the broad basis of their social edifice, which could only be built up in territorial concentration on the traditional soil of their ancient Kingdom: Palestine. Colonization he defined as an elementary stage. He foresaw that a capitalistic crisis was rising on the horizon, and he clearly saw that the Jews, being a minority everywhere, would be its first victims. He therefore stressed that the Jewish middle class should mobilize its capital to develop Palestine, and in this way create a demand for Jewish workers. With Jewish working masses in the country the basis would be established for a steady development towards a Jewish Socialist State.

Today, after two world wars and the victorious achievements of Soviet Russia, these doctrines seem to have jumped hurdles decades ahead of their time. . . .

Incredible, something hard to comprehend. Such an intoxicating idea. "Colonization he defined as an elementary stage." To think, the Jewish rich will help construct a state that will, after its founding, do away with its original benefactors, the Jewish bourgeoisie? *This* is class struggle? *Colonialism* is the road to liberation? How could people be so tricked, so painfully befuddled?

"It's not even a question about should the Jews be in Palestine," I continue my response to the Zionist student. "Jews have always been there, Jews are there now. The oppressed develop wisdom, and the Palestinians put forward the wisdom of Jews and Moslems and Christians living *together* in a democratic state, not a religious one. They're talking about equality. They're *not* talking about pushing the Jews into the sea.

"So now the Zionists end up fighting against equality. What an irony—for Jews, of all people! They wanted the Jews to be 'normal' like the other nations. Sure, OK—but there're all kinds of 'normal'. Is torture 'normal'? Is apartheid in South Africa 'normal'? Is refusing to let a family return to their home or to their own land, is that 'normal'? Or is it 'normal' to fight against oppression? Is it 'normal' to want equality, freedom?

"What would the prophets say to such a state of affairs? Would you end up calling them 'so-called Jews' for telling the truth?"

"How can you say such things?" my questioner finally interrupts. "Zionism *is* Judaism! Even at the end of the Passover Seder people say—for centuries—'Next year in Jerusalem!'"

"No, Zionism is *not* Judaism—though they'd like you to think so. When Zionism first began in Europe and America, many Jews were against it. Religious people, many of them, thought this social and political, this secular movement was a blasphemy, a regular religious abomination. Even today very orthodox sects exist which think that the state of Israel is a profane thing because the Messiah hasn't yet arrived to set up a Jewish state. Reform Jews rejected Zionism, on the whole, because they were worried that the loyalty of 'Americans of the Mosaic persuasion' would be questioned. All kinds were against Zionism—Rabbi Berger, Moshe Menuhin—for a whole range of religious and political reasons. Democrats and socialists and communists, they rejected Zionism because they wanted the right of Jews to stay in their lands and to fight with all people for democracy and social change. Even many people in the Zionist movement itself—like Martin Buber, Judah Magnus, Albert Einstein—called for a binational state and not an exclusively Jewish one. There have been so many Jews with so many different ideas—how could you possibly say that Zionists equal all Jews? You might not like these ideas, but all these people were Jews.

"But, like you say, 'Next year in Jerusalem....' But *which* Jerusalem? You want to go to the Jerusalem of conquerors and oppressors? How about the Jerusalem of American-style condominiums? I'm not interested in that Jerusalem. All those years the Jews mourned the loss of Jerusalem—maybe some people were interested in setting up another kingdom again, I don't know. But the way I understand it, 'Jerusalem' took on some religious, moral, and ethical meanings along the way. Powerful, universal meanings. You know, *not* a nation like the others, meaning not conquerors and oppressors—the Jerusalem of justice. That's the Jerusalem I'll go to. I'm not going to the other one. Do you think a *Jew* could go to that Jerusalem? Maybe a Zionist, but a Jew?"

I feel like I'm losing it, getting sucked into wholesale emotionalism. I pull myself away from the podium and sit. My mouth is dry, my heart pounding. I feel like crying. This is the first time I have ever spoken like this to a crowd. I can feel the anguish as my blood is caged in my bones. I feel like screaming. So much pain—and so much yet to come.

I can see their combined looks of consternation, anger, arrogance—and blinding fear. "Any moment Israel may come under deadly attack by the Palestinian terrorists," the looks in their eyes say. "Children killed—blood—never again such unspeakable horror. . . ." But it's a fear that keeps blind to the endless attacks upon the Palestinians. Israel is an armed camp, every kibbutz a frontier fort, everyone a target of bitter war. Do you think I like war? You think I'm telling you this because I want to see Jews killed? You don't think I remember Hitler?

"You must be very courageous," the Palestinian student told me as we drank coffee before the program. "Among the Jews so influenced by Zionism you are seen as a traitor." I shrugged; I don't think I'm particularly brave. What could be more Jewish than to be exiled—and from my own people no less? Is it so brave to be a Jew?

I remember when I went to Israel, my Bar Mitzvah present from my parents. I was an ardent 13-year-old Zionist. I cried when I read *Exodus* and wrote a book report that earned an "Excellent" and a tree planted for me in Israel by my Hebrew school. The Hebrew language I was too lazy to fathom, but the history I drew in deeply.

The tour bus stopped at the border at the Gaza strip. It was a period of relative peace; the Palestinian movement had not yet fully evolved. In Hebrew school the 6th graders had lambasted the Arabs by shouting the mock pro-Arab slogan, "Guns for the Arabs, sneakers for the Jews!" and laughed uproariously. It's just the opposite from our little joke. Imagine the Jews running? It's well known the Arabs, backwards and cowardly, left their shoes behind in the desert sand, so afraid were they of the embattled Israelis! We are a people renewed, no longer cowering. This land is a refuge for heroes!

The tour walked to the border. Desert sands stretched all ways. My hands gingerly tapped the barbed-wire fence. Several hundred feet away was another roll of barbed wire, the Egyptian side. Between the two fences stood a small tent surrounded by sandbags where a United Nations soldier sat by his machine gun. His helmet, the bright baby blue of the UN, blazed out like some strange blossom in the scrub and sand.

I notice some Palestinian kids across the border staring at the strange-looking group of American Jews. The oldest is about my age.

She has a can of water balanced on her head. Smiling, I wave. She whirls around and grabs one of the smaller ones by the arm, stalking off, not looking back. I drop my hand, my feelings hurt and confused. The tour continued, visiting kibbutzim, the wonders of Tel Aviv, and the rest. It was a small incident, hardly to be noted, describing nothing really of the issues. But for years I was haunted by the girl on the other side of the barbed wire. Why did she turn away?

"No," I told the Palestinian student over our coffee, "I don't think I'm especially brave. I'm just doing what has to be done. There are others, and there'll be more." I felt a little *too* casual. Was I just patting myself on my back by way of tremendous modesty? *Will* there be others? Am I some kind of fool, sticking my neck out? An adventurer?

Now I watch these Jewish eyes telling me I am the demon, the self-hating 'so-called Jew'. The Palestinians are patiently explaining things despite the antagonism. I feel exasperated, watching them fend off snide remarks, groans, and blatant inanities.

Embarrassed, I squirm in my seat, imagining I can explain this disgusting display to the Palestinians. "I'm sorry, perhaps you don't understand them, they're so afraid—"

The Palestinian of my fantasy breaks in, "Afraid of what? Afraid of being colonialists? We were afraid when they came; we spoke our fears in 1936, 1948. We fought, and still fight—against the Turks, the British, the Zionists, even against our own petty Kings and Sheiks. We're afraid, and a sadness grips our hearts as well. Our vineyards, olive trees, villages, our Jerusalem, all taken. From their fears, from their fantasies, they concoct the 'Return to the Promised Land.' That's their analogy, their illusion. For us the reality is closer to the 'Return of the Crusades', for they came to conquer and to steal. And then they have the gall to say we don't even exist, to say there are no Palestinians. No, this they can't take away, this we carry even as far as San Francisco. We too cherish our Return, but we will return to a land where we will share with the usurper—that is our offer! Can they expect more? It's not as if we can't see the pain twisted in the eyes of the Jew, for we can, the same as in ours. We can also see the rifle butt in the hands of the Zionist. . . . "

"But it's just like the Vietnam War, they're the same. At first they're for it, then bit by bit they understand and change. I saw it before."

"Good," my fantasy exclaims. "Then change them!"

"Huh? *Me? What're you, nuts?*"

Fortunately I'm only arguing with myself as the forum draws to a close. It will take so long to convince—and the progress of the problems unfolding, the Palestinian Arab and the Jew actually building a world together, will take such hard bitterness, such suspicion, such blood.

As the audience leaves, a student approaches me—Jewish, interested, filled with pained inquiries, open, and perplexed. It is a joy to see that we had some effect.

"Do you ever go to Temple?" he suddenly asks.

Puzzled, I reply, "No, not really, I don't consider myself religious. Though I love the prayers, the music and their feeling. . . . " Ah, still he harbors suspicions this Jew may be "so-called" after all. He has his checklist, some way to touch base. Anyway, I suppose a simple answer is adequate.

"Do you ever sing the Shma?" Do I ever sing the Shma? Well, I suppose I do, it's a powerful song. Should I say "no" just to show that the truth of what I'm saying holds firm even if I never step in a temple in my life? Why does everybody want some kind of credential, a special covenant stating that the bearer herewith. . . . Ach, it's not such a big deal. This Jew is not at all "so-called."

"No—well, yes, I do, I sing it quite a bit actually. I like it. *Why?*"

Sweat-lodge

Hot—my lungs on fire, my hands, knees,
burned alive, hunched in an oven—
scalded, crouched, naked, crowded with others knee-cap
    to knee-cap,
sweat-lodge hot rocks so close my scrotum retreats.
I slap my shoulders to cool them as the sweat-lodge
    leader prays,
"Grandfather, remember our Indian brothers & sisters
    in the White Man's jails,
Grandfather, help us to remember the four colors of man,
help us to remember Mother Earth and all our relations. . . ."
He splashes more water on the rocks we inhale
    as excrutiating steam.
I slap & squirm as each takes a turn for prayer.
Now comes my turn to pray. . . .

What can I say?
Should I sing *Shma Yisroel?*
Hear, O Israel . . . that we are one among many?
Perhaps I am of that lost tribe now found.
By chance I came to Yurok land, landed
a teaching job—*sure, Indians, why not?*—
far from New York, far from myself, just
    passing through,
now to find myself in the heat of a struggle
of all Indians, all people.
It was just an accident.
I needed a job, that's all.
I didn't realize it would come to this!
To be a Jew naked in an oven, alive with fire!
Is this the Goldeneh Medina?
So much has been torn in the name of gold
that only silt remains, scars
to which I came with flowers in my hair, almost a fool,
but it is everything that we've known before,
massacres that have come before.
I am the evidence of Eastern Europe.

By accident I fell in with Indians
to become American, become a Jew
reaching to yank the thorn in my refuge.
No, I don't want to be Mojave, not Sioux.
I want only to share justice,
to exhale the steam of the honor of peoples,
of all our relations.

The rocks wait for my prayers.
What can I say?
I don't even believe in God!

Finally my heart opens plain words
after all my inner jumble, & I gasp:

"Help us to work harder to free all
activists from the FBI frame-ups."

The sweat-lodge leader splashes more steam.

Aiiee! I am not Jew, they are not Indian!

We are all hot breath!

It Is Not Forbidden

It Is Not Forbidden

The family was small, my father's side almost entirely murdered. My mother, my mother's sister, and their mother had survived; they were the family as I grew up. There was always a feeling that something special by way of horror marked us, something hardly ever actually spoken of but referred to constantly.

My father and mother had returned to Poland in 1938 to convince the others to flee. Both families refused, my mother's because they were patriots, my father's because they were pious. After all his family was butchered and gassed, my father in anguish and rage renounced all religion, that stubborn piety of his father. After the Nazis, his father was to blame. Every Yom Kippur my father would close his business but would not go to shul; instead he would sit in his chair not saying anything, watching TV.

Now I have a cassette held in my arms like a baby as Rosa tells me her story. We tramp from shopping center to shopping center, passing endless lawns and garages, kids on bikes, and gardeners who are mowing and sweeping. I've come to Long Island to hear my Aunt Rosa tell me her story of the Holocaust. The confused, painful, and vague sense of horror I felt growing up I would this time capture on Memorex. This time I would fathom it.

Rosa is still energetic, explosive, dynamic. She talks incessantly in English accented by remnants of Polish, German, French, Spanish—all the languages of her wandering. At 60 she still looks beautiful. Ah, she was young in Warsaw before the war, the darling of the cafes. A Jewess, but her father was an official in the government; she didn't even know Yiddish. The story rolls out, hour upon hour of it. The sycamores of Valley Stream turn into the ruins of Warsaw under siege. She waves her hands, and the people walking their dogs stare at us curiously. Her father was second in command to the Mayor during the siege of Warsaw. Defeated, her father died, sick, but still fighting. Bodies blown up on the streets. She nurses the wounded. Then the ghetto walls go up. She works as a waitress in a cafe of artists in the ghetto. A German film crew follows her as she walks in high heels. *See, the Jews are not bad off after all, keeping so stylish!*

The Nazi sees her aunt, sick in bed, and says, "Poor woman, just like my own mother, let me put you out of your misery," then shoots her through the head. The Umshlagplatz fills every day, the cattle-cars crowded. One line to the left, another to the right. One line to death, another to the brush factory to work. Rosa steps to the work line. The Jewish policeman says, "You have no papers, go to the other line!" "I want to work!" The Nazi asks what's going on. The Jewish policeman says she does not have any papers. Rosa is beautiful. The Nazi looks at her. "She looks strong, let her work." "But, sir—" "Let her work!"

A commotion begins downstairs from their apartment. She runs down the steps. "Are the Germans going to clear out the building to the Umshlagplatz?" she asks an old, bearded Jew who has been agitated and yelling. She asks in Polish, and he stares scornfully at her, so beautiful, so assimilated, and he answers in Yiddish. She runs upstairs. "Mama, what does this man say? I don't understand." Her mother shouts, "Who said this? Who put this curse on you—'May you die amongst the goyim?'" But Rosa thinks: It's like a message from God! *That's* how we'll survive, amongst the goyim! Then the Germans come. They slip out the backyard, her mother still clutching the pot of kroopnik, barley soup, and out of the ghetto through the sewer to the Aryan side.

Rosa finds papers, a job at a German laboratory. She inspects food packed by Poles for the front to prevent sabotage by poison. She looks through a microscope. *How they squirm!* At night she shares a bed with a white-haired Polish teacher, the bombs falling on the ghetto, crying so she will not hear, such a nice little woman with white hair, every night the bombs on the ghetto, and the teacher prays, *"Thank God, they are killing the Jews!"*

She works in the laboratory, she eats, everything is safe, it's Christmas even, and the Germans invite her to a Christmas dinner. There is the Gestapo, even the woman Gestapo, the scientists, secretaries. At the head of the table sits the doctor, behind him big Hitler on the wall, and the soldiers serving them, and they start to serve them drinks. She is saying things she's not supposed to say, dangerous things. They tell her to sit down, one Gestapo always looking at her, suspicious. By that time she has bleached blond hair, her eyebrows plucked out. But that Hitler on the wall is bothering her a lot. She begins to say in Polish, "Why doesn't he drop dead?" "Shut up!" the doctor says. "Sit down." The Gestapo keeps looking at her. "Do you know some songs?" "Yes," she says, "I do," and what does she sing?— *The Polish anthem!* The doctor throws her out of the room. "Never do that again, they will *kill* you!" But she was so beautiful, he gave her money, told her to run away.

In Spain they were burning books, auto-da-fe, it was Inquisition, but even in Inquisition time if you decided to be Catholic they left you alone, they let you be, but with Hitler it was no way. If you say *Yes* I want to be Catholic, I want to be Protestant, I want to be *anything*, I want to be *Nazi, just leave me alone*, I want to be *fascist*, there was no such thing, they were the first race above everyone else. In the time of the Inquisition it was a question of religion; in the time of Hitler it was a question of race. Just a pretext. Poland had a terrific agriculture, Ukraine too. Germany didn't have any food, they were congested, they had no colonies, they couldn't expand, they used all kinds of pretext. The Jew was very convenient.

Rosa talks on as we stop in front of a Grand Union supermarket. Cherries are for sale.

She wanders in the Aryan section, sleeping in abandoned buildings, no papers, frantic, starving. When she was in the Aryan section she was an outcast, that feeling of an outcast, that you are *pariah,* that you are not allowed to do anything, that you can't go *nowhere,* you cannot drink coffee, you cannot knock on the doors, you cannot talk to people *maybe they know you are a Jew,* feeling of an outlaw, till the end of the war—.

The shoppers notice the strange couple out front, and I hustle her off down the residential streets.

Finally she gets captured purposely as a Pole to be sent to forced labor. She is sent to Germany to a box factory to make boxes for ammunition. All the time sabotage, they build the boxes so when the bullets are put in they fall apart, but you can't tell who or why, all the time sabotage. All the time the Germans yell faster faster. She marries a Pole for convenience, it's better in the camps. A common criminal, he wants sex, she says no, he beats her. "I know, you are a *Jewess!*" he shouts with sly venom. "I will inform on you unless—." And she sneers, *"And if you do I'll say you knew all along and you tried to save me,"* and he turns white because the punishment for helping Jews is death. They have an uneasy "marriage." But together they run away, escape into the woods, eating grass, stealing fruit, are captured and sent back after beatings, torture.

They begin to suspect her. She gets sick, and they place her in a hospital, give her truth serum; French POWs come by to tell her the Germans know she's a Jew. Weak, she jumps out the hospital window and runs again into the woods, wandering. Starving, after weeks, miles away, she turns herself in. She says a different name, she is lost from her group, wants to work. They take her to the big Gestapo headquarters, they torture her day after day. *"Tell us the truth! Jewess!"* At night the other women in the cells treat her wounds. Delerious, she is about to give up; her will is broken. A woman, a Pole, undresses her, tears her own brassiere and panties, with cold water compresses her body, all blue. She whispers to her. "We know, don't give up, everyone gets this treatment, *just don't give up, don't admit nothing,"* but Rosa moans, "I don't care, I don't care." "No no no," the Pole says, and Rosa regains her hope. They slam doors on fingers . . . a Russian soldier has the skin from the bottom of his feet peeled off and they force him to walk, bleeding. . . a British officer parachuted behind lines is captured and quietly waits for the firing squad . . . the Catholic priest is immersed in ice water up to his neck. The Polish woman is taken to slave labor and sure death; she leaves with her fist raised up. Finally the rest are taken to another prison. The next day the Americans bomb their old prison, killing everyone left behind.

They put her to work on a farm. There is so much bombing, the Americans are coming, she hides in the barn. Finally the tanks are coming, she jumps out with a white sheet waving, shouting. *At last!* The tanks keep shooting, ignoring her, and she ducks. The next day the Americans set up their administration. She wakes up and opens wide the window, stretches, arms wide. *"Free at last! I can't believe it. I survived!"* She hears the click of a rifle cocking behind her. She whirls around, a Nazi is aiming at her, vengefully. *"Jewess!"* But an Italian also working on the farm jumps him, beating him and beating him again until his head is crushed in. . . .

Sneaking on board barges and trains pressed into service by the victorious allies, Rosa makes her way from Germany into France. At last she disembarks at the Gare du Nord in Paris—at last, Paris. She has only one thought, to come to America, as she is swept into the sea of French and British and American soldiers.

"Who are you?" some soldier asks, astonished to see the beautiful and disheveled woman among them. "Rosa—I come from Germany— forced labor." She hesitates, then adds, "I am a Jewess." The soldier's eyes widen. "But we thought all the Jews were dead!" "As you can see, I am here!"

Suddenly the soldier shouts, "A Jew—alive! She's alive, the Jewess is alive!" And for a moment Rosa chokes with fear. In the great railroad station, filled with the tumult of weary soldiers traveling home, the cry gets taken up. "She's alive, the Jewess is alive!" And they hoist her up on their shoulders triumphantly, parading her through the khaki-filled station. Rushing into the streets, they march past poster-crammed kiosks, sidewalk cafes filled with laughing Parisians; past thin trees, they push by the cabdrivers honking and the official jeeps waiting against the curbs; wild with joy at the end of war, they laugh and drink, all the time shouting, "She's alive, the Jewess is alive!" until military police finally pull her down. Even in peace, perhaps she is not safe in the company of a thousand drunken soldiers, and they send her off to a relocation camp. . . .

We finish for the day our hours of retelling terror. "Why don't you go to a movie, relax?" my mother suggests. "Go see *Manhattan* with Woody Allen, it's good." Rosa and my mom laugh and chatter about the movie in Polish and English. "What did he call the mother, a *something* mother?" "A . . . a, a something mother? A crazy Zionist?" My mother laughs. "I can't remember exactly, but it's good. It's playing at Green Acres."

I walk across long parking lots. It's not often I go to the movies alone. I feel slightly in shock. It's so impenetrable, the Holocaust, imagining the depths of fear, horror. I remember the way my aunt described herself when she first came to the US. "I was talking with blood, I couldn't sleep nights." A comedy is fine, ease my mind, ease the moral imponderables so I don't talk with blood.

A cartoon. Ah yes, Woody Woodpecker . . . but I grab the armrest in alarm. Woody is a cowboy being chased by a big hulking dumb Indian; they cat-and-mouse across the screen. Woody plops on a headdress, sits in a teepee, and offers the dumb Indian a peacepipe. He winks as he pours gunpowder into the bowl and watches as the unsuspecting brave lights the match. *Boom!*

Hey, who's writing this book anyway? Did somebody know it was me sitting at this movie? Is this a plot, some scheme? The cartoon gets worse and worse. I start groaning, imagining sitting in Berlin watching a movie of a Jew getting his beard yanked off. *Ha ha, what a riot!* America has surely taught Europe the real meaning of Western Civilization.

My heart aches and lightens only when I realize no one is laughing, and others join me as I boo at the end.

Then, without a pause, big sweeps of Manhattan skyline, the suave dreaminess of George Gershwin. Woody Allen and Woody Woodpecker? A stand-up comedian has been let loose upon the West Side chased by elegant neuroses. At least he doesn't like Nazis. Naturally I laugh . . . Jewish intellectuals, the art of self-deprecating humor. But I want Charlie Chaplin, he was a shlemiel with a little dignity hearkening of ancient glory and loving kindness. *The Maimonides of comedy!* The Jewish comedian—Mel Brooks, Lenny Bruce, Groucho—forms a new Rabbinate on the road to assimilation and modern disjointedness, a real wisdom. Everyone loves it. See, we're still chosen for something!

But, Woody, what are you doing? Everyone in the movie is white, wealthy but not too wealthy, an artistic type, liberal, George Gershwin sweeping up Broadway. *This* is New York? What happened to Puerto Rico? Is Harlem still uptown? Suddenly I realize what the whole movie is—it's a lengthy, fascinating advertisement for the *gentrification* of Manhattan. You know, every decade or so it seems there's a switch in who actually *gets* the Urban Core, the poor or the rich. It looks like in the '80s it's, "Welcome back, nice folks! Sure, you can still get mugged in Manhattan—but it's *Manhattan!"*

Woody, is that what all this sexiness is for? *I should be neurotic for a loft in Soho?*

I come home after the movie, drained. My mother asks me, "What did he call his mother in the movie? Crazy Zionist?"

"No, he calls his mother a *castrating* Zionist." My mom cracks up, tickled the joke's on her.

"But, Mom, you think *that's* funny? Let me tell you about the cartoon. . . ."

My aunt's story still unfolding, I pack up my cassette to talk with Palestinians. In a simple matter of time and space, a silent whirling box sits on a couch between me and Ghassan Bishara. In minutes an intimacy is formed that, without this Panasonic, would otherwise take years.

Ghassan is a correspondent for a Jerusalem Arabic newspaper. He comes from a village near Maalot in the Galilee and grew up as an "Israeli Arab." His village was bombed in '48 but his family took temporary refuge close by, not in Lebanon as those thousands did who linger yet in refugee camps. He went to Jewish schools, spoke Hebrew fluently. When Israeli Jews from the Ministry of Education would come to his village, they used to bring him to talk to them to show them how the Arabs could speak Hebrew. It sometimes became beneficial and profitable, actually physically better, not to tell that he was an Arab.

The settlement of Maalot is built on his village land, and the Arabs used to go work there. You had to have a military pass to go work in the settlement. In order to have a pass you had to cooperate with the military government and be their friends and tell something about your brother or your mother or your sister or your uncle. Some of them didn't want to do that. He didn't have a pass, like many of the others, but a lookout on the road would signal if police were coming.

Boom, the lookout yelled. They all disappeared. Ghassan also ran, behind some wall where he was urinating when one of the police came and caught him and said, "What are you doing?" "I'm working." "Are you Arab?" He said, "No, I'm not Arab, I'm Moroccan Jew." The policeman, very tough and a big tall man, took him around to a Moroccan Jew and asked, "Do you know this man?" The Moroccan spoke to him—he knew a little Moroccan Arabic and was just going to answer when the policeman yelled to another Arab from a different village, "Hey, do you know this man?" "I know him, he's from the village there, and his father's this and his mother's this." The big man looked at the boy, smacked him such a force, again and again, until he ran.

"I ran miles and miles from him," Ghassan explains in an agitated but self-controlled manner, "and I was running and thinking that he's still behind me and eventually I get back to my home—but this I also remember well: that I denied my identity for one, and then that wasn't good. I get hit also for it!"

Hilton: One of the things I'm doing in New York is interviewing my aunt. She survived World War II, and one of the ways she survived was to pose as a non-Jew. The same situation happened to her, more or less. "Are you a Jew?" and she didn't have papers or anything, so she shouted indignantly, "Who are *you* calling a Jew? I ought to turn *you* in!" Because she was assmilated Polish and she didn't even speak Polish with a Yiddish accent, she was able to pass. A lot of times men if they did that they would simply pull down their pants, see if they were circumcised. At that time the stakes were instant death.

[To Ghassan] You look Arab the way I look Jewish. You've got blond hair, light skin, and so on. You could speak Hebrew, you could pass.

Ghassan: Definitely. I passed many times for a Jew. In school in Jerusalem I was in love with a Jewish girl. She was Moroccan, and really we were very much in love with each other. When her parents found out about it, her brothers knew she was dating an Arab, I was actually physically threatened that if I am to be seen again with their sister I would be killed simple as that. We continued dating each other, but very secretly.

I wasn't really welcome as an Arab into who I considered to be my Jewish friend's houses, and this really was saddening to me. I always claimed that had the Israeli government treated the Arab 'minority' in Israel very well they may have succeeded in turning us '48 Arabs, making us see the other side of the creation of Israel. But we were treated as second-class citizens, a hated unwelcome minority. To be treated equally wasn't in their plans, even on an individual level.

I don't know, philosophically speaking maybe the world expects too much, maybe we expect too much of ourselves. We think that because the Jews have gone through such experiences that they should not allow it to happen to another people; they know how bad it is. But then again maybe we are expecting too much. Maybe people are naive . . .

Hilton: It shows for me that things can turn into their opposites. Those who have been oppressed can become the oppressors, that's a very powerful lesson. Maybe the oppressors can be, not against the oppressed, but part of the liberators also. That'll be a great day.

Ghassan: I tell you, I really hope so. Also, I don't think all the Israelis are oppressors; not all those who have been oppressed at some point are oppressors now. There are many Israeli Jews who have no part in all of this Zionist-racist-fascist stuff.

To many of them, coming to Palestine is really a logical escape. Maybe they didn't have anywhere to go, maybe that was the thing to do, and maybe had it happened to the Italians they would have done the same. Now that the Israelis are there, the Jewish people in Israel are there—Palestinians really do not doubt that at all, they know it's a fact—they don't dream or think for a second that we can now do to them what they have done to us. This is really a far-out, unacceptable, unthought-of solution. The best solution is to get together in a secular, democratic state. Many of the leaders of the Palestinian revolution are thinking along these lines.

Hilton: When you speak about a secular demcracy, one of the fears that a lot of Zionist sympathizers have is that Jews once again would be a minority, in particular in the Middle East, surrounded by a hostile Arab world. When you consider the situation of Jews in America, where Jews are currently a minority, there's an inconsistency of logic. How would you approach discussing that with someone having those fears?

Ghassan: I had a big interview with Uri Davis, who is an Israeli anti-Zionist activist, a few months ago, and we had a big discussion about this issue. First of all, there are minorities in the US, and I think the Jews are a minority here. Although anti-Semitism *is* an issue—there is no argument at all about that; in the US there is dislike for Jews—I think there is—

Hilton: But not on the level that there is dislike for Black people or anti-Semitism in Eastern Europe.

Ghassan: That's right. But it's really interesting. From time to time I would be talking to Americans and they would know I am Palestinian, that I am sympathetic to the Palestinian issue, I have more than once a chance to see the ugliness of these individuals, because they think if I am Palestinian I am anti-Semite, anti-Jew, and they really open up to me, and I'll tell you it's so ugly, it's so bad, it's so disgusting. Not everybody, but there are a few people. I sometimes have to let them know I am not a racist, and a racist is the worst kind of a human being there is.

But being a minority, if a secular democracy is established in Palestine, being a minority in itself is not really bad, *if* the state can guarantee the rights of all people, including of course the minority. The history of the Middle East does not have systematic hatred, racism, and discrimination. I personally think it's a Western invention. There *is* discrimination in many countries, but the discrimination is not really against minorities. *Nobody* has rights. The state is the owner of the people, taking away rights not only from minorities but from all of the people.

So in Palestine, I think and I hope and from the philosophy that the

Palestinian revolution is spreading it will not support anti-Semitism. This topic Uri and I were talking about, and he said, "But I am an Israeli Jew. I did not immigrate here by my own choice. I have some attachment to the land—not Zionist attachment, but I was born there. What would happen to me?"

My best answer, which he accepted, was, "Jews can have their cultural independence in Palestine, in a secular democracy. A state should not interfere in the cultural affairs of any group of its citizens." It's not a hope. I have talked to many Palestinian leaders, and they are really convincing individuals. The answer to them is secularism, democracy, socialism. I know to many Jews, many Israelis, this answer, they would say, "Oh, you say this, how do we know?" Well, it's true, you cannot know. How can you guarantee something now?... But I'll tell you, all of us young Palestinians, if there is a Palestinian state and I see any hint of anti-Semitism or anti-Christianism or anti-anything, my struggle will have to continue. The state many of us Palestinians are struggling for is not for another semi-pseudo-democratic-pseudo-socialist secular state. We have so many in the Middle East we don't need another one. I don't know if that answers your question.

Hilton: Well, it answers it for me. There are no guarantees; the only guarantee is to struggle for it. My own opinion is that for the well-being of Jews in Israel the best allies the Jews have for the long term are the Palestinian people. Not the US, because the US, when its interests change, will do what it needs to do. I know, given the current situation, such an idea seems strange. But there would have to be a transformation, a revolution, in Israeli society to make that break.

"What?" Rosa shouts, "*You think the Palestinians are the best friends of the Jews?* You believe this Yasser Arafat? Oh, now I didn't think you were such a stupid boy, so naive. *George Habash is a Zionist for Palestinians!* When they take over, they will not allow the Jews, not at all. Don't be so foolish."

I try to reason with her, play some tapes of conversations with Palestinians. Despite my Memorex diplomacy she stands unmoved.

"I believe the Jews are a nation, a nation with a religion. Saying the word *Jew* is the same as saying *Israeli*—only that we happen not to live in Israel so we are not Israelis; we are Americans or French or English or Germans. Any nation should have country, the Jews should have country. If you leave them alone they are not attacking nobody. If they attack southern Lebanon or any part, it is when their colonies or their towns are attacked. *They give back!* The Jews learned one thing: From now on, after Hitler, Jew will never die just waiting till he is killed. *He will kill!* I agree with everything Israel is doing, if they have to attack and kill, *even if they use atomic bomb*, if any moment should come because of petroleum or whatever, the Jews would be isolated and left on their own and with economy terrible bad what they have and no help, not being able to survive and maybe attacked by Arabs en masse. I agree with *anything* they do as long as they survive. They have an army, they are existing, they can attack, they can trigger Third World War, they can do something or die in honor for their country!"

Israel takes on the appearance of an oversized Masada. Resistance by suicide is popularized. Israel stretches out like a mighty Samson *Clone Golem* between two columns of the palace. Samson's hands are tied to the US on one pillar, and to the Soviet Union on the other. Desperate, the hero cries out, "Let my soul die with the Philistines!" and he pulls down the whole palace, dragging the rest down to doom with him.

I feel my insides tearing apart. This investigation is starting to become more like open heart surgery. I realize, with the experiences she's had, her orientation, it would take a lot to convince her.

Rosa laughs, "I would say if we were chosen I wish God would never choose *us*. They could choose anybody else as far as I'm concerned, because to be chosen to be killed all the time, to have a repetition, is tiring . . . *no?*"

Just down the block from the Museum of Modern Art there's a book party. A friend's novel has just appeared, and I'm coming to do honor to the Bar Mitzvah boy as well as hob-nob with New York literary lights. In a beautifully appointed flat we are served great drinks and hor d'oevres, all kinds of wonderful, tantalizing *treyf*, like bacon wrapped professionally around liver, chubby shrimp, etc. I'm tipsy like everyone else, listening in on sophisticated and witty conversation. *My God, I've walked right into a Woody Allen movie!*

A pleasant woman introduces herself. She works at a soon-to-appear new women's magazine as an editor, which, she explains, is very exciting and meaningful. "What do you do?" she asks me. "I'm a writer too," I answer unsurprisingly. "Oh? What are you working on?" "I'm working on a book about Jewish identity in America—poems, stories, essays, a series of things in a, uh, kinda personal serious Woody Allen vein, uh . . . from an anti-Zionist perspective. . . . "

Her eyes widen. I realize she's Jewish, that I may have to run for my life. Ah, but this is a university-type crowd, and she confides in me. Of course the Zionists are fucked up, but you should know about the Arabs too. I lean closer, we're getting serious, confidential. I grab a shrimp from a passing tray for company. "Every nationality has a *sexual pathology*," she explains. Every nationality has a *what?* "Everyone does, naturally, but you should be aware of the Arab's pathology. What they have done to Israeli soldiers is bestial. When they are captured, wounded, the Arabs mutilate them, cut off their genitals and eat them!"

I don't say anything. Paralyzed. *Maybe this little story's true? What's the point?* With a jerk I offer her my shrimp on a toothpick. She declines.

"Really, when you're doing your investigation you should remember this. They definitely do *not* have a Western orientation."

"Uh, yes, they certainly don't have a Western orientation."

My aunt is not a castrating Zionist. She is strong, defiant, fun-loving, shrewd, emotionally gushy. Ever since she came to America (stopping over for ten years before moving on to Venezuela, then returning) she did not feel quite comfortable. America was wonderful, but the Americans, they have no culture, no feelings. "They hear I lived through the war . . . I had a few men ask me, 'Were you raped by the Germans?' They didn't think about they were killing, putting the gun to the head, just splash the brain outside, they would not think of the gassing, the first thing what they had in mind was were we raped by Germans. So this in itself was very disgusting. Besides, Americans, they were not interested in hearing about the war. Those that came back were the victims of the war, they would understand. Those that were here were making big money. The youth wouldn't even believe; they thought we were exaggerating. . . . "

Always, the struggle remains in the questions. Who will listen to the story? Who will discover what it means? I feel those questions inside me, growing, branching into other questions.

Will Rosa listen with belief and comprehension to the stories of Palestinians? Will she hear when a student tells how, on the West Bank, the Israelis made a sweep, picked him up, put a hood over his head, beating him for days? They threw him in jail with no charges for a year until, for some reason, they let him go, still uncharged. He goes home. The Gush Emunim settler types are roaming the streets with guns. They are demonstrating for settlements. Marching down his family's street, they notice the Star of David carved into the woodwork of his house, a symbol of friendship along with other symbols from many years before. "This is a *Jewish* house! What are these Arabs doing in a Jewish house? This is theft. Move out! *Out!*" And the mob breaks into the house, forcibly dragging furniture out. After much fighting the mob backs off. Finally the military grudgingly agrees, the documents show the house has been their family's for generations.

The tall woman who was a teacher near Bir Zeit is suspicious when I ask her questions. The cassette this once doesn't bridge the distance.
    "Did you ever meet an Israeli anti-Zionist?"
    "No, no," she replies, "we don't trust them, no, no, we don't try to be friendly with them. That's what the government try to do, be friendly with them so people outside say OK, they can live together under Israeli government. We never get friendly with them. Most of them are soldiers. You don't get friendly with the enemy . . . "
    "Could you conceive of Jewish anti-Zionists?"
    "Only here in the US. Why . . . are you Jewish?
    "Yes, you didn't know that?"
    "No, I thought you were Christian or something. Oh, of course when we speak about Israelis we distinguish between Jewish people and Zionists."
    I stiffen a little. Does the distinction matter to my aunt? Sure, the characterization is correct, and fighting for that distinction between Jews and Zionists has been a wisdom obtained by the Palestinian revolution. It's not been easy. Years before, I viewed a screening of a new movie about the whole question with an audience of whom many were the Palestinian folks who ran various mom-and-pop groceries in San Francisco. As the movie traced the rise of Zionism, it showed Hitler's genocide with revulsion and compassion. But when Hitler's wildly gesticulating oratory was briefly flashed on screen, a number of the middle-aged in the audience cheered. I winced on my red felt seat. *Was the seat drenched in my own blood?* I understood, perhaps, their feelings: The enemy of my enemy is my friend, and so on. I can imagine many Palestinians who have never seen an anti-Zionist Jew, couldn't conceive of such a thing, so the distinction becomes almost irrelevant. But I've also seen the children of the Palestinians in that audience who, red-faced, argued with their parents to change.
    I look at the tape recorder whirling around. Is it a cassette that

forms bonds? No, hardly, not at all. Intimacy is formed by risk, by struggle, not by magnetic tape.

"But we never give up," the schoolteacher continues, "no, never, never give up. We have a government now, the PLO, with schools, with hospitals, a government that takes care of people, with an army. No, we never give up.

"But," she leans towards me, "I interview you now. How come you become anti-Zionist? What does your family think?"

It's been growing for a while. It looks like I'll have to go to Jerusalem, see all this in its subtle and obvious designs. The Zionists call it aliyah, *a Jew immigrating to* Eretz Yisroel, *the Land of Israel. The Land of Israel stretches from the Sinai to the Euphrates. There is a lot of territory to be "liberated." A lot of settlers who are needed for this manifest destiny.* Aliyah *means "going up." For a Jew to come to Israel he is spiritually going up, they say. Up to metaphysics. I think I will become a* Yored, *one who goes down. When I go to Israel I will have to see what is really happening, in all its flesh, bones, the relations between people, Palestine. I'll be going down, down into the world.*

And what does Rosa think? My aunt has been molded by the Holocaust. And, in a way, so have I. Still, she dreams of Poland, of going back, although she knows what she dreams is done with, gone. Her Zionism is shaped by Polish nationalism still, a likeness. She could like these Palestinians. She could see the bond. Would she discover it?

"Sam Stanton is going to be a rabbi in Fiddler on the Roof? I can't believe it!"

"You better believe it," Johnny flips back. Johnny is Sam's dad, a building super and house-mover, and a writer.

I'm visiting Johnny in Yorkville, the upper East Side. Huge apartment buildings cater to the young executive, while down below in the old 5-story walk-ups the working class stays put. New York in all its congestion can often offer cross-class neighborhood simultaneity. Woody Allen is contemplating sexual pathologies on the 20th floor while down below Sam Stanton is holding court at P.S. 151.

The neighborhood is German-Irish; uptown a few blocks it's Puerto Rican. Sam is graduating sixth grade; it's the graduating class play. "It's a multi-national cast of thousands," Johnny jokes.

An ancient school building, walls cracked, fills with screaming kids and smiling parents. The lights go down, a girl reads a little introductory speech inaudibly and the curtain goes up with Sharon Quiñones, a pillow stuffed in an over-sized shirt, playing Tevye. "Tradition! Tradition!" the cast sings out.

I scan the program, look at the faces. Rodriquez, Gomez, McDermott. Latin, Black, German, Irish, Chinese. I don't see a single Jew, not a one. I panic, feel alternately alone, exposed, proud, confused, delighted, perplexed. A materialist Yored doesn't have to journey so far as Palestine. New York opens its arms, a Golem built by a Golem. In New York, Eastern Europe is a part of grammar-school mythology like Pilgrims wearing funny hats and Peter Stuyvesant's big buckle and peg-leg. Puerto Ricans as Jews? Why not? The Golem built by a Golem takes the people of the world, digests them, spewing forth a working class. Jews, we've traveled a lot, we should know. We should be *nationalist* for America? Plymouth Rock is the Rock of Zion? To be a class-conscious Yored in America is a big job yet to be accomplished this time around. It's a powerful thing to have the peoples of the world on the stage of P.S. 151.

The people of the village break into dance. Suddenly the very modern boy asks a girl to dance. "A man and a woman dancing *together?* It is a sin, a sin!" Sharon Quiñones stops the dancing, "Let us ask the rabbi!" "Yes, let us ask the rabbi!" the villagers chorus.

At last Sam gets his chance. Short, in a blue suit, a cardboard hat wobbling on his long blond hair, a black beard painted on his face, he looks perfect as a Pennsylvania Dutch. With a gigantic grin and a sing-song Jewish accent that sounds more like Chinese, he belts out, "IT IS NOT FORBIDDEN!" and sits back down on his wood bench throne, triumphant. The village dances in joy.

It is not forbidden.

Kamal Boullata is an artist and writer from Jerusalem. In 1967 he was in Beirut when "Jerusalem became further than the moon overnight." After wandering without documents through the Middle East, the Quakers gave him a grant to come to America where he resides, all the time traveling back and forth to the Middle East. But not to Jerusalem, even with American citizenship. Nor is it a question of danger.

Kamal: It's strange, but I don't think I can take it emotionally. I have seen people, members of my family, and it's been devastating for them. The only thing that hasn't been destroyed yet is my childhood memories of Jerusalem; everything else has been. So, if I can retain my memory of Jerusalem—and I'm not speaking of a celestial memory or a spiritual memory, but a very terrestrial memory of a place ... perhaps in that way I am very much like the first Jew who dreamt of going back. But somehow I don't feel ... I try so hard not to fall into the temptation of wishing to go back to Jerusalem, because I can see that the Jews went back, and they were faced with a reality they couldn't deal with.

In 1973 I wrote a poem, and then later it was developed into a whole vision, a series of paintings, in which I spoke of the concept of the Return and made an analogy of the return to the womb of the mother. But Palestine is a lover; it's going forward, it's not going back.

Hilton: There's been a lot of comparison between the Jewish Diaspora and Ghourba, the Palestinian dispersion. How do you think that has affected Palestinian people in a broader sense? How do you see it affecting you in America, that transformation?

Kamal: I think it is very easy to make analogies and to make parallelisms. It's even cute to do that. One has to be very careful about this, because the concept of the Diaspora had a great deal of spiritual quality and a longer historical background than the concept of the Ghourba which the Palestinians have been feeling. The very word Ghourba comes from the roots for "westwards" or "sunset"; it also means "something on the other side," it means to be alienated. It has so many concepts that are rooted more to Arab culture than they are rooted to a general Western way of seeing things. All that I can say about this is that through my Ghourba I was more able to understand better what the Jews have gone through in their Diaspora. When I first came to America here I was with Quakers, and I went back to rereading the Bible. It was the first time the words from the Psalms, "O Jerusalem, I will never forget thee, let my hands forget their cunning, let my tongue cleave to the roof of my mouth,"—it never meant so much to me than when I was in Pennsylvania reading that.

I have painted Jerusalem, I have known every street of it, I remember every stone of it. I'll never forget a recurrent dream I used to have right after the '67 War. I would dream I was in the middle of a narrow street in the Old City of Jerusalem. I was like a child and there was a curfew. All the shops, all the houses were closed, and all of a sudden I would hear the thump of an Israeli soldier's boots coming down the street. I would turn around and he would see me and then start running and he would be following me and he would be running and he would shoot and I would feel the blood running on my back. I would be thinking that no matter what would happen he would never be able to find me because I know Jerusalem, the alleys of Jerusalem, better than he does.

When I have read about Jews in ghettos in Europe, about their dreams, their paranoia, I can see all the seeds of what Jews have gone through in history are being sown in a new people. So the parallelism is there constantly in the personal lives of the people, but it's a luxury for us sitting here in America thinking of it in these terms. People go through these paranoias or fears; they don't have the luxury to make the parallelism. Sometimes I'm reminded of a proverb in Palestinian colloquial Arabic that says, "He who takes the blows is not like the one who counts them." This proverb comes from the people that has gone through taking blows and has felt that others may be counting them. But one cannot be masochistic either in one's thinking. Instead of counting blows one can stop them . . .

Hilton: How do you see Jerusalem being rebuilt in reality—not that it isn't reality inside of you also—but how do you see the next stage of struggle with Zionism? Do you have a vision of what that new Jerusalem would be?

Kamal: I cannot visualize it, I don't have the political vision to see that. I think the so-called new Jerusalem would only be there if each one, whether Jew or Arab, Christians, Buddhists, whatever, would be able to deal with what is within in terms of memories and in terms of dreams. I can see many parallelisms about the memories of Jews and Palestinians about Jerusalem. Are the dreams the same? What Jerusalem? It differs. And as long as there are human beings that think Jerusalem is only *mind* there can't be a new Jerusalem. There will only be a divided Jerusalem, and Jerusalem will remain a dream.

Hilton: It's such an irony that Jerusalem has become such a symbol world-wide; it's just a town.

Kamal: It's a very strange city. If it wasn't for its geographical location, let's say, it would not have had this very historical importance. Then there were other things that were combined of natural elements such as water in that area, such as air, the climate of it. When you think of all these elements that combine to make this place, you can't help but think, whether there were religions there or not, it was destined to be that way. Even if time were to begin now, that place is destined to be fought for and to be loved and to be died for.

Hilton: I recall reading in Europe in the Middle Ages they referred to Jerusalem as the navel of the world.

Kamal: Yes, the navel of the world. The world was divided into three sections—Asia, Europe, and Africa—and Asia was a triangle on top and a dot was in the middle. There is a church next to the Holy Sepulchre which is called "Heart of the World," meaning like the axis of the world. All Christian Arabs have these legends on an everyday basis. I never realized how much in my own upbringing as a Christian in Jerusalem there were so much pagan things in my own culture of everyday life. I'll never forget, for example, around Spring, when Eastertime is near, the hills of Jerusalem would be filled with bright red flowers. We used to call them "The Blood of Christ" around the Holy Week. Then I realized this is what used to be called "The Blood of Adonis" at the time of Jeremiah, and here we carried it through our Christian Arab folklore . . .

To me Jerusalem is the faces I lived with, Armenians, Copts, Assyrians, with ancestors that go back *also* 2,000 years ago, who pray in their church in the language that Christ spoke when he was around that area; they also have 2,000 years of history, Abbysinians. These are Jerusalemites, Arab Christians, Muslims, Jews. This is what Jerusalem is, the interaction of all these faces, and these people who love and fear and interact, who speak broken Arabic and who speak half Armenian and half Turkish. That is the humanity of Jerusalem to me, not only stones and monuments as if it was an archeological dig that was recovered after all this loss underground, as if the human beings on top are only a mere obstacle in the way of archeology, the way so many Israelis see it.

This is where the tragedy is, where a stone becomes more important than a human being. I say the next Jerusalem must be human, the next Jerusalem must be new . . .

No, it is not forbidden. I suppose none of it is forbidden. Out of the horror, the violent juggling of history, a resolution is anticipated. Maybe I'm getting dreamy about the Messianic age. Maybe this is the Chosen Planet, an entire Planet. Or maybe I can see too clearly the modern-day idolatry of commodity fetishism in America, in Jeru-

salem: the things, and not the relations between the ones who use those things, becoming gods. The people have become the property of all these gods, these delusions, and the universe is sliced, divided, parceled out. Didn't we have this argument a long time ago?

The tape runs out. The "eject" pops up, and the cassette skips out of the box. Hours of talk, my investigation swaddled in plastic boxes. I've hardly begun, the relations, the history so complex. Should I compare the relative merits of different forms of torture on a scale of 1 to 10? Does Dachau rate 10 and the Palestinians rate a mere 4? Does 20 years in a refugee camp equal one day in Auschwitz? It certainly isn't a perfect equation; neither is it essential. The pain of the Holocaust is unbearable. Yet its story, its summation, its meaning is not done with; now Israel is the false murmur of its meaning. The Holocaust walks the Galilee.

Surely I am considered a traitor, this "so-called Jew." Perhaps I'm like the old mystics who see a mitzvah, a blessing, coming from what appears, on the surface, to be a transgression.

Palestine—and America too—is a transformation whose seeds have been planted thousands of years before. The flowers will blossom on the hills around Jerusalem some day. It will be a day when all the Yordim of the world, the people who fondle dirt, machines, and paint-brushes, will take the shrines and reinvent them. Jonah will jump out of the whale, and the people of Nineveh will exclaim, "Where have you been? You've fucked around so long we've done it ourselves!" And the hills of Jerusalem will then be covered with bright red flowers that we'll call "The Blood of the People."

It is not forbidden.

The Jew that Julius & Ethel Carefully Shepherd & Bloom

The sons of Julius & Ethel Rosenberg
listen to the radio:

The Lone Ranger suffers villainy at the hands of enemies
who fling false accusations against the Masked Rider
of crimes unknown & unbefitting the friend of grace & justice;
how rapt the sons of Julius & Ethel listen, so greatly relieved
when the plot is exposed by the clever deduction that,
while the silver bullet recovered from the scene of the crime
could be squeezed between the teeth—thusly—
the silver of genuine heroes would remain hard—like so—
proving that the Lone Ranger was the victim of . . .

How stubbornly the boys click the radio on as the FBI
    clicks it off,
off, then on, the agent off, the boys on
until Ethel's anguished cry,
"I want my lawyer!"

How rapt they tune to the radio
as Mommy & Daddy face the Jew judge & Jew prosecutor
    with Jew defense team
for the "crime of the century."
How casually, walking across 51 St. Manhattan
as I visit from California decades later,
do I learn, at last, of my grandfather's post in the
    Polish government:
Ministry of Interior, Criminal Division.
A socialist of sorts,
yet he was enlisted to lead
surveillance of Jewish Bolsheviks.
"He was a decent man," my mother said,
"and he saved many Jews, socialists, secretly. . . ."
I'm sure he did.
Perhaps he would save me.

"Go ahead, try to save the world," my father exclaims.
"You're young, and you'll learn:
It's every man for himself, out for himself.
You have all your friends, but wait till you're sick;
wait to see who visits you, and you'll see.
No one gives a damn, and they forget you like that.
No one wants to be around anyone sick;
they have their own business to attend to.
No one will pay the bills for you.
I don't care if it's Russia or Cuba or America
it's the same, it's—"
My mother butts in. "My cousin in Krakow
she's a Party member, a true believer, you know what I mean,
and not a real Jew
and even she says the Party members get the cars and
     good pay.
She doesn't like it but what can she do?"
(My cousin? Another in the family like me? I never knew!)
"So stop this foolishness to change the world—
Yes," she pounds the table, "the Jews are out for themselves too—
     good!"
"Ach, let me finish—are you done? Can I speak?"
My father, out of the embattled citadel of his small business,
his ark that he himself built in the ghetto of textile
     merchandising,
my father sighs, "Go ahead, try to save the world,"
because he has seen iniquity and death
and he has no other answer.

Julius & Ethel wait in their cells for the electric chair,
communists, common Jews, like so many others.
The execution is set for just before the Sabbath evening.
The rabbi makes one last effort to coax their "confession."
They can save themselves if only they name names.
"*Nu,*" I can hear my grandmother pipe up,
the Yiddish wife of the very Polish patriot
who slid out the sewers of the Warsaw Ghetto to escape,
"they say we killed their baby Jesus,
they say we bake our matzoh on Passover
with blood from goyisheh babies,
so now you should go ahead and steal the Atom bomb?

What does a Jew do with the Atom bomb?
Tell them what they want to hear.
Give it back!"
Yet, again, Julius & Ethel spurn the false accusation.

Mother, father, all of you,
don't be upset, don't worry:
I am the Jew you brought me up to be,
the Jew that Julius & Ethel carefully shepherd & bloom,
the Jew of history, who changes
steadfast like Julius & Ethel,
the Jew who visits the sick and spurns lies,
who burns Treblinka to the ground,
who embraces the Palestinian,
cries out against iniquities
because of love,
the ex-Slave of the Royal Treasury who wanders,
who binds memory
to the small experiences of one life
so the story becomes a guide,
who stumbles over the ghosts
trying to tear a purpose
out of hard rock,
the ex-Slave yet to be free,
the Jew who isn't even a Jew
yet who is a Jew,
who becomes—
          "OY!" my mother screams,
"he's a communist, what else?"

I am the Jew that Julius & Ethel
carefully shepherd & bloom
as they sit in their cells on Sabbath eve.

A Conversation with Simon Ortiz

"That's a powerful story, a powerful book. It's so unusual—I think, in America, there's no comparison," Simon remarked about this writing as we sat in the cool shade of the small one-room stone building behind his mother's house. "You said you were out in northern California working with the Yuroks. Was that under the Teacher Corps?"

Simon Ortiz had witnessed the birth of this book. Now Simon, Acoma poet, teacher, and activist, was showing me and my companion around Acoma Pueblo. He explained the uranium mining, how the people farm, the challenges the people face today, the changes that have come about over many years of foreign domination—first Spanish, then Mexican, and now American.

People have lived in Acoma for a thousand years, more or less. Only for a little more than a hundred has the Pueblo been ruled by the United States as part of New Mexico.

The Pueblo itself stands on a sheer mesa overlooking a wide expanse of land. To the north, Mt. Taylor, sacred to the Acoma, Navajo, and the Mexican *penitente* sect, reaches high, a mountain containing some of the richest known deposits of uranium in the world. In comfortably furnished offices atop faraway steel mountains, giant energy corporations maneuver to rip out Mt. Taylor's guts. Already, down one slope the Jackpile Mine gapes, a huge gouged-out cavity. It is one of the largest open-pit uranium mines in the world.

We had walked by a crowd of tourists being shown around adobes and stone houses by a Pueblo guide. They looked like displaced persons from a shopping center. I felt lucky to be a friend of Simon's, to avoid suffering embarrassment in the company of tourists. Later, though, when I visited the Taos Pueblo, I had my dose when a Texan, barging through a curio shop, asked the old Indian woman at the table, "Where are the scalps?"

Years earlier I had approached Simon, who was living in San Francisco at the time, to collaborate on a project. We would each write a series of pieces based on the theme "How I Came to California," trying to evoke an understanding of the social as well as personal forces involved in propelling people, whether that be flight from anti-Semitic Poland or relocation egged on by the Bureau of Indian Affairs. At the time we mulled over how California worked as a magnet for many peoples, and we hoped to encourage other California writers to explore their own histories in such a light.

We both avoided the question almost entirely. As I worked on the project it became this book. Simon, likewise, embarked on another plan. His question changed into "How the hell do I get *out* of California?" Eventually he moved back to Acoma, completing a book of poems on the local history of uranium exploration, how the people saw it as it grew to its present monstrous proportions. It's a serious look at views by the Indian and non-Indian workers in that industry called, simply, *Fight Back*.

"How did you get to teach on a reservation in northern California, anyway?" Simon asked. Ten years earlier I had come to know Indian people as a schoolteacher in a Yurok village on the Hoopa Indian Reservation. At the time I hadn't thought I was embarking on a journey to understand so many complex relations. I never expected to sit, ten years later, in Acoma talking about it.

"No, that was a regular State of California school district. I needed a job, we were broke, I didn't really think very much. The woman I was married to at the time and I decided to live in the country. We wanted to flee what was happening in America in 1969, the Vietnam War. So when we were passing through Eureka and we heard about that job, we thought it was just living out in the country and, sure, all we had to do was to teach people . . . ha! It was actually one of the hardest things I ever did. We were so foolish, I can't believe it, to be so naive. But it was a kind of age that we were in and the circumstances where you just throw yourself into it. What we wanted to do was to throw ourselves as far away from what we knew as we could. And it was . . . it worked. But we weren't motivated by any great moral 'help the Indians'. We just thought it would be a nice place to live."

"Unless I'm wrong," Simon continued, "my perception of it is that a lot of young people, especially young Jewish people, who came out to Indian reservations, were basically very innocent in the sense they did want to help—for some it was maybe an escape. Their social motivation was not just derived from where the oppression was happening—*here*—but from another source. If it was back East they transferred that out here.

"I remember the first time that I ever met any number of enthusiastic, excited, young Jewish people was out at Rough Rock on the Navajo Reservation. They were college students who came out during the summer of 1968. I was a teaching intern at the high school, teaching Navajo history. You're talking about being caught up in an age! Here's me, an Acoma person, going out to the Navajo reservation teaching Navajo history! And they, coming from New York and other places back East. We were involved in community work. The Navajo people at Rough Rock were wondering what we were up to.

"A bit earlier in the '60s they had also come out. Since they had skills and education, they usually landed in positions of administration, writing proposals, sometimes getting in tight with tribal councils. They took over oftentimes the direction of tribal programs because of their education and their ideals and enthusiasm. Sometimes this was detrimental. But I say innocent at the same time, because I think they didn't really know what their particular use was, what the motive of the capitalist structure that put them there was. And that the Indians would still always be down below.

"But one of the things that kind of made them attractive, and at the same time also maybe awkward to work with, was how they wanted to become so much a part of the community, wanting to throw away whatever values that were identifiably screwy and negative in many ways, and take upon themselves what was 'down to earth' or 'grass-roots' or 'native', which led to a lot of funny situations, sometimes very distracting. So I just wondered if in that sense you came to California?"

I felt somewhat embarrassed. My experience, in many ways different, is still very much a part of that pattern. "We wanted to be in the country, and didn't know anything about Indians," I replied. "Romantic ideas about 'back to nature', 'living with the Indians' type of thinking, were very quickly dispelled trying to teach. The kids basically were trying to tear the school to pieces, and there we were in that situation trying to keep the school intact, not knowing how to teach and going to district meetings where all they talked about was bus routes and insurance policies. It was pretty obvious we were teaching there because they wanted to collect Federal money into the school district and they needed somebody in that isolated two-teacher school to take attendance for them; they weren't interested in the quality of the education. The people knew it; it was pretty insulting. If they were going to hire untrained people they could've hired someone from the community. But being white, having a degree from Columbia College . . .

"Though we did basically have a moral stance that it was a good thing to do. We wanted to go live some place isolated, to get away from America, but during the course of teaching we really got the overwhelming sense that we had not gotten away at all. We were right in the center, the heart! We realized there was this nice school building surrounded by a cyclone fence with a little flagpole, no electricity in the village though the school had a generator, the only radio . . . we were running it like a community center also, with volleyball once a week, movie showings . . . and every day I was supposed to raise the American flag on our hilltop overlooking the village. We were operating an outpost of the US government, a 'fort'!

"There were a number of good things we did, we tried. The only way I could assess it was that at least we never got 'deviled'—people in the woods trying to spook us with curses. People thought we were young, trying to do our best. When I visited the teachers the next year, they knew how to teach, but they didn't know how to relate to the people, less than us at least. The man was saying how he wasn't going to talk to some guy because he was a drunk. I told him, "You can't talk insultingly like that. You're going to get into difficulty with the people." That couple ended up getting a truck driven through the plate glass window of their house, their two pedigreed dogs poisoned, all their guns stolen, their car totally destroyed; they were deviled and run out. They knew how to teach—and they were very good teachers —but they didn't know how to relate to the people. By negative example it was consoling to us.

"Basically, when that experience was over, I was really glad to leave. But I had learned an awful lot. I learned to respect the people for who they were, but it was not at all romantic. It was at least one layer of romanticism, of paternalism, peeled off, though not the last. No one in New York could tell me how groovy the Indians were."

Simon prods me more. "But I've often wondered how it was, particularly to Jewish people, because they say they're the ones with the most experience with oppression of any white group. This is the thing on the surface most observable maybe, because so many of the white people who came out here were Jewish young people. Sometimes they were hippies just passing through, wanting to help or something; not having any way to help, they were both searching and rejected at the same time. I don't think it was just the Jewish propensity for endurance, but it seemed to be part of the innocence or something that led to some identification with the oppressed, who, of course, were the Indian people."

"That's very real, Simon, because of the anti-fascist history, because of World War II and consciousness about the Holocaust. Even before, the Jews who were recent immigrants to the US at the turn of the century were very socialist inclined. But even within the culture, the religion, the history, there's been a long thread of knowing oppression, of fighting oppression, and of humanitarian moral standards;

though that doesn't prevent other, less progressive, threads emerging and dominating also. There's been a long history of resistance which I try to speak to. You could take the Prophets or Moses. You could look at Jews as ardent supporters of the French Revolution, fighting for emancipation. The Holocaust. That's definitely been an aspect of it. Yet, considering the degenerating effects of Zionism and the rightward drift of this country, I don't know where this trend will go now. I hope this book helps to keep the tradition of justice-seeking strong."

"Well," said Simon, "in the civil rights movement the motivation for it was an understanding of what political oppression was, and then what the economic basis for that is. The kind of help that Indian people wanted was basically skills that we could use. Indian people always were suspicious of missionary religious people. At least the Catholics in this area already had it all sewed up, and priests, of course, wanted to protect their territory.

"Jewish people who came here, young people, were not selling religion, so that was attractive. If it was Mormon youth who came or Southern Baptists or something, they would usually have their book open in the first ten seconds. They were always wanting to convert you. But the Jews were not selling religion. They were usually selling politics."

"That's the new Jewish religion—ha!"

"Really," Simon continued, "it became very informative, maybe somewhat speedy for many Indian people who had been oppressed for so long, wanting to know. The '60s for Indian people was really a decisive point. We were not totally ignorant; we knew what we needed. And perceptive people—not to lead, although this did happen, and this was resented when white professionals, as I explained a while ago, got in the administrative positions, became planners, and to a large extent, they still are. It was very hard to get around that or to throw them aside. Blacks and Chicanos eventually did throw their white organizers out to a large extent because of this. Some of it was just plain old white arrogance; a lot of it was the position they were placed in. For Indian people it was oftentimes, 'Well, the BIA and OEO and HEW are not gonna listen to *us*. Therefore, why don't we get us a guy in a suit and white skin?' That was the rationale for them.

"From your own experience, even though you were a principal in a small school, that was partly your role, as a kind of facilitator. How did that make you feel, being in that role? You talk about this, of course, the Jewish role historically. . . ."

Again, why did he pinpoint me? I felt surprised, though I don't know why I should've been. I'd said all this myself.

I collected my thoughts to reply. "In some ways it's similar in terms of being a middle-person. I don't think I did a very good job, that's one thing. The main way I had to do it was, for example, when some things would happen and I had to call up the Sheriff's Department on the radio, so it was like calling the *cavalry* to come down. Someone's house got broken into, a lot of times the kids were involved, family problems, a kid was sent to a BIA school because they decided he was too unruly to take care of, so I had to appear at hearings and testify. I'd have to deal with what was going on in the community, and it was so contradictory I couldn't get a handle on it. . . . "

Oh yes, so contradictory. . . . My mind flashed to what some of the parents said about disciplining their own kids, "The only way to keep these Injun kids in line is with the paddle—that's the way the old teacher did it." Confused, I scoffed at such ideas at first. Me? I was just going to do the best I could at teaching.

Years later I learned the cardinal rule of teachers: "Be strict at first, then lighten up. Otherwise, kids, after they test your meagre limits, will walk all over you." My attitude then was more akin to: "Golly, kids, I'm just folks. Let's be reasonable and talk about how we can work things out. I'm just here to help and—" Pow! They walked over me like I was the main road to Eureka.

After two weeks I was desperate. Colonization doesn't make it any easier for the "noble" agent of colonial power. I thought twice about the disciplinary ideas of those parents I had earlier scoffed. What else could I do? The kids were literally kicking holes in the walls, tearing the place to pieces. My ounce of youthful, white authority was ridiculed and under siege. Maybe these parents spoke with some wisdom. After all, it's their kids, they ought to know.

Tiger was the oldest boy, the most disruptive. I decided that when next he acted up I would, after suitable warning, let him have it with that paddle left behind by the old teacher. Naturally, he played right into it. "OK, Tiger. Come with me into the principal's office!"

"Ooo, Mr. Openzipper gonna really do it! Ooo, Tiger!" the girls screamed.

Tiger walked into the office adjacent to the classroom.

"Bend over, Tiger. Grab your crotch," I said, according to the instructions of the bus driver I had called in to witness as stipulated by regulations. Tiger bent over the short-wave radio as I gave him a few half-hearted swats with the paddle. The bus driver smirked as he leaned against the wall, chewing his Chiclets.

Tiger just laughed and sauntered back to his seat. Denying all pain, he displayed great 7th-grade manhood. I followed behind, desperate as ever in the face of the uproar. So much for this great white father.

After school was out I drove up the dirt logging roads that went along Pecwan Creek. Completely in tears, I lurched, talking to myself, hysterical. Logging trucks were careening downhill as I pulled off into the turnouts, sobbing. My personality had split into two, and I was arguing with myself, screaming, "No no no, I don't wanna do this, I don't wanna hit kids—but I have to . . . I don't know what I'm doing . . . what's going on? *I didn't come to the middle of the woods to end up hitting kids!* No!"

Finally I made it back to our house, resolved that I'd quit before I'd hit kids again. I didn't do either, eventually plugging ahead as best I could.

So now Simon was asking me these questions. We'd talked before. He knew my story. But he was prodding, gently nudging the thin tissues of self-righteousness overlaying memories. Once, foolish and young, I ran the "fort." Quietly, unconsciously, I wandered into a role set aside for me in America, and no easy conversation could bridge the river I had had to cross. . . .

"On the other hand," I explained to Simon, "Alcatraz was happening, and so I tried to bring things, pictures of Indian leaders of the past, tried to have older people come in to sing, to talk. When Alcatraz happened, I remember saying some things about it, and the first response was one of the kids, Tiger, saying, "Aw, they're just acting like a bunch of niggers." *I* was there, so maybe that was a response to *me*. Anyway, at vacation time I went to SF, picked up bumper stickers and posters—'Indian Power' things—and they went like *that*, they took up the idea of 'Indian Power' pretty quickly."

Simon deepened his own observations. "I know the role of white people in general, now; class distinctions are very clear. There's the people you don't see but who are the real power; they don't come here, they stay in the banks or something. The Federal policy makers also. Then there's the working-class whites who are the ones you see in town, Grants, or the miners out here. They're the ones we have most contact with in the immediate area, and we pretty much know where we stand with each other. Then there's the experts, a whole new class of technological experts who have a role with the industrialization of this area, working *with* the corporations or *against* the corporations, who are part of the Southwest now. And nobody really knows how to deal with them. You sort of need them, and then they're the ones that really are the facilitators, especially for the corporations, for the industrialization of this area. Then of course there's white people who are intermarried with the people. I guess you could class them with Indian people cause they're part of the Indian communities. Still, sometimes there are conflicts, but it's more like personal conflicts within the Indian areas."

I was starting to feel agitated. I was still up in the hills driving the dirt logging roads arguing with myself, crying. The recollection of it, here at Acoma, was painful. It was hard to be objective.

"Your investigation is personal, but it's also inclusive, especially when you look at yourself as a group, as a community, the American Jew and his role, relating it to other areas of the world and to the most immediate conflict. To make it apparent to people, not just to other Jewish people, what it means to be a Jew in America, but also what it means to be an Indian and a colonized person in the world, not just Acoma or New Mexico or Northern California or Palestine. You ask the question, how has the oppressed become the oppressor? It's very interesting; it's a painful question. Do other Jewish people ask that?"

"No," I replied. "Some do, but most Jews don't see it that way. Most Zionist sympathizers in the US—people with good hearts, most likely—feel that the oppressed have become free, that there are still enemies all over trying to destroy what has been made. For those people who have been displaced—the Palestinians, the refugees— that's perhaps very unfortunate and a sad thing, but it's not their problem. The general position of Zionists is that here is this one little Israel and here are all these Arab nations all around to which the Palestinians should be welcomed and absorbed, because they are Arabs, and one Arab is an Arab is an Arab. But the Palestinians have resisted that because the people are attached to Jerusalem the way your people are attached to Acoma. There wasn't an overall Palestinian nationality in the modern sense. That's a creation due to conditions of today, but there were always the people, and they had their sense of who they were. Today they are the Palestinians. Most Jewish people don't realize that; they hide from it or reject Palestinian national and human sentiments outright. Much of this is due to the influence of Zionists, this enforced ignorance, blindness or callousness, skillfully mixed with emotionalism.

"I'm not too familiar with other situations in which the oppressed have become the oppressors—but in a way it's similar to the Pilgrims coming to colonize the US because they were religiously persecuted. Perhaps similar to Afrikaners or with Australian convicts. There is a similarity in which the process of colonization—settler-colonialism—has involved the oppressed and lower classes to serve its purposes."

Simon described the present controversy between the Navajo and the Hopi over disputed lands. Both peoples are being manipulated to see themselves as victims, the oppressed, at the hands of the other. Beneath the disputed lands are huge coal deposits. The manipulation is being done by the major economic interests in this country. "Of course, when that is done, when people are manipulated, being formerly oppressed, to be an oppressor, it's quite easy when there's an overall overruling capitalist structure itself...." Simon paused as we thought of the hugeness of this reversal of roles. "I've heard some Indian people really express sympathy for the Jewish state, perhaps even for Zionism. I've heard Indians say, 'Wow, look at those Jews! They got it together, *they got their land back!*' Really, sincere admiration. They were really admiring how hard they fought."

"Yeah," I explained, "there's definitely an aspect of that which, in the early '50s especially, won over a lot of people. Plus Israel had a progressive, egalitarian image, with social innovations and socialist type stuff. But have you spoken to those Indian people about the Palestinians being the Indians from whom they took their land back?"

Simon chuckled, "I think there are people who are aware of that now. I don't hear very many pro-Zionist Indians nowadays."

We talked of the possibilities of the future. Next year, 1980, would be the 300th anniversary of the 1680 Pueblo Revolt. Simon explained how, after a hundred years of the Spanish colonial yoke, the people unified and threw the invaders out in a clean sweep. For twelve years they stayed free until, divided and weakened, they were reconquered by a search-and-destroy strategy.

"Do you know what the relevance of the 1680 Revolt is today? *It's that struggle is against oppression in general.* The 1680 Revolt was a multi-cultural struggle; it wasn't just a Pueblo fight. By the 1680s there were class distinctions among the Spanish. There was the royalty, the ruling class; then there were the people who had intermarried with the Indians. Black slaves. Then the different Indians themselves, all at the same time. Today, when we talk about the uranium, what the land is, what kind of roles that people as racial groups or cultural groups are put into, we need to understand how we are used against each other. How we need to overcome those roles.

"Pueblo people were used against Navajo and Apache people in the nineteenth century. The Mexican people a lot of times are still used against the Indians. Among the Pueblo people there are those who work with the government; they don't have to rely on migrant labor or mining work or stock raising or subsistence farming. The government selects these people who have some training, some education, to be put in this position. It's really hard once those people get in those positions to know the process that is at work, which then divides the people further."

Simon had volunteered to help his uncle build a new house, so we drew our conversation to a close. He had some last thoughts as he went rummaging around for a wheelbarrow.

"What strikes me about your book is a growing awareness of the role a group of people, in this case the Jewish people, in the settling of an area; how that role is used by the rulers of this present system; and what that makes apparent to other people. Indian people are really getting stuck, going to get stuck, in that role. Somehow, our struggle for sovereignty must not be pushed into that role where it becomes a weapon against the larger America, the *potential* of America that we can have. I don't think that Indian people want to be just used like that. If that should happen, we will always be discriminated against, always be objects of racism. But, really, to work for some really well-founded nation that recognizes people . . . there's more of a chance for true sovereignty, sovereignty with all its economic self-sufficiency and political freedoms. This country—not in its present way—this nation, this people can achieve it. And I think a book like that really points up this potential and possibility. . . . .

"I don't know what your readers will get out of it. I'm sure the Zionists will have hanging parties out for you!"

We laughed. Simon walked out to our car with his wheelbarrow to say good-bye. I was dazzled by the New Mexico sun, the bright mesas, the dry heat. It reminded me of the Holy Land. It was time for me to go home, back to California.

"Simon, I hope you build a strong house for your uncle."

Batiks by Lisa Kokin

The Golden Land — די גאלדענע מעדינע –

Ellis Island

The First International Women's Day, 1908

פֿאַר מײַן טײַער טאַטע,
דו זאָלסט לעבן
נאָך אַ 65 יאָר
געפֿילט מיט געזונט און גליק,
מיט אַ מזל ליבע דײַן ייִדישע טאָכטער.

Zeyde: A Portrait of My Great-Grandfather

"For my dear father you should live another 65 years filled with health & happiness with love from your Yiddishe daughter."

Rebbetsin.

Inspired by a poem by Aurora Levins Morales

Loteria de la Vida: Portrait of Frida Kahlo

Remember Ethel and Julius Rosenberg

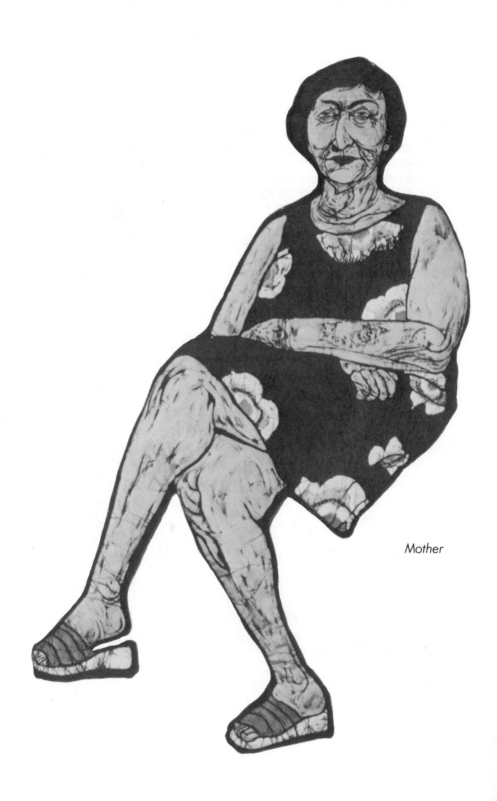

Mother

The Palestinians: We Shall Remain

Tal Al-Zaatar, 1976

Jewish-Palestinian Solidarity

Haggadah

Is It So Bad?

Lisa picks up a tool that stretches down her finger and at the end of which sits a small copper cup. The tool is called a *tjanting*, from Indonesia, and the hot wax drips out its spout and onto the cotton cloth her finger runs across. She's filling in a background for a batik, her hand deftly dabbing between the cloth and an electric frying pan that holds a hot, clear puddle of wax.

After sketching with wax for a while, she pins the cloth across the doorway, and, by standing off to one side, we can see the color flashing through, how the dye will cast. It's a portrait of Felix Ayson, a Filipino Manong who lived in and fought for the survival of the International Hotel. For ten years the elderly, aided by the young, especially the Asian young, fought for the right to inexpensive housing in what remained of the first Filipino community, Manilatown, dating back to the '20s.

For years the hotel stood with the huge financial buildings of San Francisco's downtown looming just overhead. They were like sleek, computerized UFO zeroing in on the old three-story brick bulding on the walls of which a large yellow-, black-, and white-striped tiger had been painted. The tenants, mainly older people, predominantly Asian —the elderly immigrant bachelors, the ex-busboys and farm workers —organized and gained the support of students, housing organizations, and a broad range of political groups. Hemmed in by discrimination, the Hotel was their only home. Tucked into the edge of Chinatown and the Broadway redlight district, filled today with topless/bottomless joints, and the encroaching highrises, the hotel was as tenuous as their lives. They had nowhere else to go. The Hotel wasn't lovely, it was necessary.

Toward the end, by the middle '70s, the demonstrations against its demolition filled the streets with up to ten thousand people. The investors had plans for yet another highrise Mother ship to tower over Chinatown. The International Hotel, just down the street from the white heights of the TransAmerica Pyramid, became a center and a symbol, a challenge to *all* the investors.

When, after the final court order, after the final meeting with the mayor, even after the sheriff himself went to jail rather than carry out such unpopular enforcement of private property, when the late-night eviction came with the combined troops of the sheriff's and police departments, something felt in the heart hurt terribly.

Felix was in his eighties and had been deaf for years. Yet he always held animated conversations by way of penciled messages handed to him to which he would respond slowly but eloquently. "We are not just fighting Four Seas Investment Company, but a whole class" or "As yes, Hilton, and how is Wounded Knee?" Old, he was finally receiving the attention anyone craves, though he was only one among the hard-pressed tenants. He loved the limelight he was held in by the young, perhaps more than he should have, but to them he was a permanent example of the will not to give up. Not long after the eviction, exhausted, he was dead.

In the sketch on the cotton of Lisa's batik Felix is standing outside the door of the Hotel in front of a poster of the Hotel's tiger around which "Defend the International Hotel" proclaims: "Rally to Stop Evictions." Many times he would stand outside the door of the Hotel leaning on his cane with his familiar green Army cap on his head.

After the waxing is done Lisa dips the cotton into a big photographer's tray of brownish dye. A bulky gas mask is clasped around her face, and her hands are protected by large industrial rubber gloves. In a while the batik is hanging over the shower-curtain rod, the brownish dye dripping atop the bathtub wall and splashing across the bathroom. Sometimes her roommate leaves little notes on the telephone message pad that read, simply, "The bathtub is full of dye/and you will die." Sometimes it can be hard. I can see the sign up on an index card in a bookstore: "Woman roommate wanted to share flat with other women. Must be able to live with hot wax and dye dripping across bathroom floor. Nonvegetarian. Smoking OK."

I glance again at the brownish dye splattering across the floor, at the metallic showerhead. A frightening half-thought shoots across my mind, and I whirl around. *No one slams the door airtight, not yet; no one slips me a cake of stone soap.*

Relieved, though embarrassed at my persistent paranoia, I ease out into the hallway once more, comforted by the batiks fastened to the walls. There is Frida Kahlo, the Mexican artist, her face and upper torso like a large stuffed doll, while Tarot-like cards tumble out of her bag, each marked with a symbol of her life. *Love. Art. Politics. Pain.* And each a tiny pillow snapped to the main piece as it falls. Julius and Ethel Rosenberg sit at home for a family portrait that now hangs like a large quilt. Women work in a field in Mozambique, bent over into the shape of a warm pillow.

A warmth in Lisa's batiks adds tenderness to zeal—a humor. I wouldn't mind tucking myself in bed with the Rosenbergs, or resting my head on a pillow of Africa. It's such a woman's art, I guess, this tradition of quilting, except now it's done with Indonesian dye technique and a Jewish eye. Lisa doesn't like to sew, despite the long tradition. She'd much rather have a machine, if a machine could do it right and she could afford it. But one can't, so she jokingly complains. Such painstaking garment work is a Jewish tradition as well. But the warmth in all Lisa's batiks is what makes statements, portraits, and scenes alive, fresh, while the dreams, the storms people must go through, hang very nicely on the wall, apparent and strong; such power emanates from luminous yellows, deep browns, and reds. Lisa's batiks would hang very well on the walls inside anyone's life in America—though I can't yet imagine many Americans who would sit one soft evening at dusk and contemplate the face of Felix Ayson.

Appropriately, however, these are the walls of America. Appropriately, her themes range across the world. Chile. Nicaragua. I see a Jewish great-grandfather with a beard and an inscription to Lisa's father in Yiddish: "In honor of your 65th birthday, from your Yiddisheh daughter." And another, the image of a Yiddisheh daughter shaking hands with the daughter of Palestine, a rifle slung over her shoulder.

Continuing to walk through Lisa's rooms, I view more faces and scenes. Lisa has started to people the walls of her house with images of being a Jew. She tells me how she came to it, and I recognize the same dynamic as my own. For years she couldn't think about it. Considering her identity in the light of her uncomfortable yet vague feelings about the state of Israel kept her at a disquieting distance. She explained that she chose *not* to think about it, afraid of the turmoil and conflict that would rise up, even though she was outspoken about the Vietnam War and racism, the women's movement, Chile. We were part of the same youth wave of Long Island immigrants to San Francisco during the late '60s and early '70s. I chuckle at our kinship. Exiles or refugees of a sort, perhaps, except that we've traveled so far to find something, hardly realizing we were propelled by some escape. Maybe we could've started our own art trend, the "New York Exiles School," except we didn't feel like exiles.

Years before, at the time of the final Roman siege of Jerusalem, Rabbi Johanan Ben Zakkai, esteemed and learned, was spirited out of the beleaguered city by his disciples through the ruse of a coffin. Both defenders and besiegers allowed the funeral to pass. Once outside the gates of the doomed city, the rabbi emerged from the coffin and made a small request of the Roman conqueror, Vespasian; so inconsequential did it seem that the request was granted. Allow him only to open a school at Yavneh, he had asked. The Prophets would still be heard; the temple didn't need walls; it was justice, salvation, and charity that Israel would disperse among the nations.

Was it justice, salvation, and charity that *we* came to California?

What is *our* school, anyway? How do we learn *our* Torah? Watching the dye drip into the tub, I can't help but think of the International Hotel, with its ironic yet accurate name. Watching Lisa at her portrait of Felix, I recall that night of brutal eviction. I remember a 95-year-old Chinese man in slippers and bathrobe hobbling with a cop at his arm; the cop pushed him to the other side of the barricade, to nothing except bewilderment and the aid of his friends—us. On horses, mounted police had charged the crowds of thousands blocking the doors. Oh, how the Czar's horses come back to awaken fresh terror! With long batons they had swung and slashed at people. I saw Wahat Tampao later that night—actually it was the early dawn—75 years old, living in the International for decades, he was bent over in the park in crowded Chinatown—homeless, spent, weeping uncontrollably. A young Filipino woman put her arm around his shoulder, holding him, coaxing him to speak, because Wahat was still the leader of the Tenant's Association. It was hard to watch an old man, a proud and athletic man, his pride shattering. But eventually he did stand up before the people, and he spoke, leveling curses at the mayor and Judge Ira Brown. And everyone wept together even as we raged.

Those crackled lines of wax expose a crumpled familiarity in the face of Felix. From the end of her pointed finger, Lisa scribes the dripping wax. It's merely wax but a wax felt deeply, colored. She is not an exile in San Francisco but a Jew. The International Hotel. One more fight where we learn our Torah.

The book has never seemed enough. The *interpretation* is the life, the learning—or the corruption. I remember laughing when I first discovered the minutes of the Pilgrims having a meeting of their new settlement in America. The date is 1640, and they discuss the issue of the land, concluding that:

1. *The earth is the Lord's and the fullness thereof. Voted.*
2. *The Lord may give the earth or any part of it to his chosen people. Voted.*
3. *We are his chosen people. Voted.*

Voted: Evict the sun, evict the moon. America is chosen. Not New England, but New Jerusalem! Voted: Divide the waters into the owners and the owned. And on the Seventh Day tabulate your election.

Pilgrims, you'd make wonderful Zionists! You too have your place in our school; from thee we learn. The lesson is in Lisa's batik of frightened faces standing at the rails of the steamship porting in America, Goldeneh Medina. It's yanked Lisa by the hair, drawn me, blasted the Arawak and Taino as they dashed against Columbus. And we know it. Now, today, that knowledge is Jewish, is American. Must be.

I wonder what Lisa would think if she were to watch me write just as I watch her dab hot wax from the tip of the *tjanting*. She could lean unobtrusively against the wall as I frantically pound the desk, pace the floor, push over chairs. She could contemplate me as I indiscreetly pick my brain as indiscriminately as I might pick my nose. And as I hammer at my Smith-Corona, she might see a gas mask bouncing on my nose; perhaps she'd notice my wax which, once hard and hidden, like hers, oozes down my fingers and on to the keys that I pound.

"How did you ever come to this, to feel these things?" she might ask.

I'd have to think, sorting out experience and dream, reality and the passionate inventions of a materialist Yored. "About 10 years ago an old man asked me a question during Passover, a Seder. He asked, 'Is it so bad to be a Jew?' Slowly, I've tried to answer his question, at first not even realizing that I was."

"Well?"

"Well, what?"

"*Is* it so bad to be a Jew?"

I half-notice Lisa as she tidies up her work room, putting her tools back in place, tossing out old newspapers rigid with wasted wax. There's nothing for her to do now until the batik hanging from the curtain-rod drains itself dry. She's got a few hours to kill and is ready for a walk, so she invites me along. "*Is* it so bad?" I wonder, absorbed.

Passover, the old man asked me at Passover. I remember it: escape from bondage; the old shepherder's ritual; sacrifice of the lamb; the renewal spliced to a Greek symposium with cups of wine. Maybe next Passover Lisa can batik the cover for the plate of matzoh. We'll have a Seder with her batiks hanging on all the walls. The idea excites me, and I get suddenly frantic as I blurt it out to her.

"But who would I invite?" I stop short. "My parents? Wahat? Aunt Rosa? How about George Habash and Kamal Boullata? My 7-year-old stepkid Kalayaan, watching the Brady Bunch? Simon Ortiz? Yeshiva University?"

"Are you thinking of renting the Cow Palace?" Lisa inquires.

"Well, OK. How about some friends?" I concede.

And then it occurs to me—the seriousness and power of the uplifting ritual meal. Passover. I would invite, at the least, all of those who for years couldn't think about it, who stayed frozen as they hid from themselves and the items of memory alive today.

Most especially, I would invite them. Those like Lisa, like myself.

Haggadah

Here, sit down, my friends. Join this Passover Seder. Sit by my table, all of you. Get comfortable. Listen to the ceremonial sequence and the telling of Pharoah, Moses and the escape from—

Look! Up over your head I hold the shank-bone. In my fist the lawyers would call it a "blunt object," with cartilage and meat dangling. Spring comes, and the People, the wandering shepherds, butcher the lamb—a sacrifice, one lamb for sacrifice, the best. *Here,* see, I smear the blood on the doorpost—*go ahead, you too*—just as they did once to shield themselves. Blood-sign to show we have avoided death again. Shank-bone in hand, it's the same blunt bone with which Moses dropped the cruel slave-driver, knocked him dead in rage. Moses fled, he reflected, his love and rage became a burning oneness, burning but not consumed, and he returned. The start of a new season, shank-bone held up—like so. Don't be afraid. The bone won't crack *your* skull—you're not the Pharoah, are you?

Pick up the leafy parsley, dip it into the saltwater of tears. Spring, the obvious, shameless revolution, has won.

So sit down. Come around the table, eat all night long. Be my guest, linger over conversation. Don't rush off, let's talk, dream of spring, the work of freedom.

Here's a toast, the first, lift up the wine: *Remember freedom,* remember the escape from bondage, a sweet wine of liberation!

Eat the bitter horseradish, the sweet nuts and apple and wine mixed like mortar, souvenirs of bitter slavery, the bricks of the masters become our own succulent pleasure. Eat the *matzoh,* the bread of farmers; not the bread of oppressors, but the bread of poor folks— *tortilla, fry bread, corn pone, peta*—bread baked in a hurry, in flight, eaten in the desert, before we became the oppressor, before we sundered into master and slaves ourselves. *Remember this simple Matzoh!* Can you remember?

But I have questions, so many four will hardly do—you have questions too—they burst out in a tumult. And the plagues? Too numerous, more than ten, hundreds. Blood spills down the Klamath, silently curls down the Jordan, a sneer; blood films over the Mississippi like an inflammable petrochemical waste. The waters divide, part overhead—will they close up over our enemies or over the heads of the people? Why is it the blood of the oppressed? Why is this stage of history different from all other stages of history? *When will we get rid of it?* Why does the Neutron Bomb with invisible hand strike down firstborn *and* last? This night, it is so different, but why? Why do we lounge and give ourselves a long meal and a meeting instead of rushing off to swing shift or to sleep, exhausted? Why do we gather to tell the story of freedom, when people are still oppressed, when the Jews themselves have divided into tyrants and rebels? *Should I tear the shank-bone from my own leg and with it beat down the—?*

But we're digressing from joy. Calm down, eat this sweet paste. Recall the moment Hitler burned. Savor the day the Shah, King of Kings, was humbled, driven off. A festival for us is a plague to the Pharoah. Eat the tasty lamb. Pick up your wine again, *this time for justice!*

They tell the story of when, in Palestine, Rabbi Eliezer and Rabbi Joshua and Rabbi Eleazar ben Azariah and Rabbi Akiba and Rabbi Tarfon were feasting Passover together in the village of B'nai B'rach. All night they talked about the Exodus from Egypt, chanted freedom, planned rebellion, studied the way. The Romans occupied the land, oppressed the people. The Rabbis plotted all night, their students keeping guard. At last dawn broke, and the activists on guard duty whisper at the door, "Already it's morning, time to recite the Shma." Time for the Rabbis to slip past the Roman soldiers on patrol.

Drink wine for the liberators, all the warriors, fighters for all people; for Moses, Tecumseh, Mother Jones, Harriet Tubman, Malcolm, Bonifacio, Ho Chi Minh, Joe Hill, Marti, for the nameless fighters of the Warsaw Ghetto and Tal al Zaatar, the numerous; a toast to the liberators, our bricks we have mixed for freedom!

But I wonder, what ever happened to the *Egyptian* slaves? How long did they labor, burdened by Pharoahs, after Moses slipped out one night in haste? How did the Jewish slaves of the Kingdom grumble while the Prophets howled?

Where is Elijah, anyway? I set his place, his plate is heaped up with lamb, his cup of wine filled, ready. Open the door wide for him. Why doesn't he come? After all, he's been invited. Perhaps he's busy. Remember when Elijah cried out against the slave-master King, Ahab? Ahab longed for Naboth's fields and orchards. How fine the trees and vineyards looked from the palace window! He sought its purchase, offering a handsome sum. But Naboth turned the offer down, explaining, "How can I sell the land? *Given by the Creator to the People, how can I give it away, sell it, or divide it up?*"Ahab's Queen, Jezebel, inveighed against his archaic thinking, his simple thought tied to a simple mode of production. What wonders the modern life unfolded, yet the fool refused! Resolved, she plotted the farmer's frame-up. Accusing Naboth of treason, she connived with Ahab to order his death by stone. With Naboth gone, the land was seized, usurped. Elijah, hearing of the outrage, boldly confronted the King. "You kill the man, you steal the land—*you* are the oppressor!" The enemy is more than the strange Pharoah, the enemy is in our midst as well, the vile Pharoah inside. But Elijah, he saw the change, he witnessed the farmers and shepherds turned off their lands, become slaves to the rich; he denounced it. How the downtrodden Jews loved Elijah, the just, our friend. He raged so mightily that even his death was a tornado of flames. Beloved, the people anticipated his return as the harbinger, the messenger of deliverance, grace, life, and peace. Every Passover we invite him in, set his place. We could use his advice. Why does he linger? Doesn't he know there is always the time and the place at our table for a hungry prophet?

I know it must be odd to see me in San Francisco, Elijah. We could go to the Mojave if you grow lonesome for desert. Do you see those gigantic palaces downtown—Bank of America, TransAmerica Pyramid? Does it remind you of home? It's pleasant here; the climate, they say, is salubrious. Much like Tel Aviv, they say. Have you seen Tel Aviv? Have you encountered the Zionists? What do you think of the new Kingdom of Israel? Do you cry out for Jerusalem?

While we're waiting I'll make another toast, the last. My friends, lift our wine in honor of the Palestinians; *may their victory come soon, and with it come ours!*

Now we're coming to the end of the Seder, my friends. We've told the story, learned a message of the Exodus for our day. We've rededicated ourselves to the cause. None of us are strangers anymore. We all sit in various states of expanded stomachs and loose belts. We're glad at last to have asked the questions. We've summed it up, so now let our actions speak. As we have celebrated this festival tonight, so may we celebrate it, all of us together, next year again, in joy, in peace, and in freedom.

Next year in Jerusalem delivered from bondage!

Of the many people who helped me as I wrote this book, I can only mention a few who talked or argued with me, and who encouraged and supported this effort: Estella Habal, Stephen Vincent, Ruthie Gorton, Aurora Levins Morales, Lincoln Bergman, Jonah Raskin, Phil Lopate, Johnny Stanton, Paul Smith, Jimmie Durham, Simon Ortiz, Kamal Boullata, Ghassan Bashira, and Penny Johnson. Thanks is extended also to the members of the Jewish Alliance Against Zionism and to the staff of the Palestine Information Office. Despite our raging differences, I would especially like to acknowledge the love and support of my mother and father—and, of course, Aunt Rosa.

Hilton Obenzinger was born in 1947 in New York. Graduating from Columbia University in 1969, he has worked as an elementary school principal on an Indian reservation, a nursery school teacher, printing press operator, and free-lance writer among other things. His other books include, *The Day of the Exquisite Poet Is Kaput*, (FITS, 1972); and as one of the poets in *Five on the Western Edge*, (Momo's Press, 1976). He lives in San Francisco.

Lisa Kokin has been working in batik for the past nine years. She has done batiks on a variety of subjects, including Chile, Vietnam, elders, Cuba, Jewish history and Palestine, southern Africa, and working people in the United States. She has exhibited widely in San Francisco and the United States.

The batiks in this book are part of a series on Jewish history and Palestine which grew out of a process of self-identification as a progressive anti-Zionist Jew.